BASTARD BLUE

BASTARD BLUE

Stories

Murray Dunlap

Press 53
Winston-Salem

Press 53, LLC
PO Box 30314
Winston-Salem, NC 27130

First Edition

Library of Congress Control Number: 2011928857

Printed on acid-free paper
ISBN 978-1-935708-33-9

For my mother and brother,
and for the unachievable wish that things
could have been different with Dad.

Acknowledgments

The author gratefully acknowledges the editors of the following publications where the following stories first appeared.

"The Ice Storm," *Barrier Islands Review*
"The Dogs Go Too," *The Bark*
"Post-War Heat," *Fried Chicken & Coffee*
"Cat Stories," *Greenbelt Review*
"I Crossed My Arms and Shook My Head," "Thaw," "Jake,"
   "Spanish and King," "Cab Ride," *Night Train*
"Neighbors," *The Hook*
"Movie Night," *Off-Course*
"Alabama," *Post Road*
"The Black Oyster," *Ptero Heart*
"60 Seconds," *Red Mountain Review*
"Night Swimming," *Silent Voices*
"Vanilla Orchid," *The Smoking Poet*
"In the Attic," "Jimbo Thames," *SmokeLong Quarterly*
"A Wolf in Virginia," *Virginia Quarterly Review*

Contents

The Ice Storm

I was born into an Alabama ice storm. So the story goes. Our family likes to say how exciting it is to be born, so small and fragile—and I am told, beautiful—into such a cold and dangerous night. Power lines snap and fall, moving under their own power like writhing moccasins. Tree branches give way under the collected weight of ice. Even the roads break apart, water filling and freezing in cracks, expanding against concrete like a wedge. Icicles fall from the eaves. One is said to have pierced the hand of an electrician in Point Pilot at the very moment of my birth.

The electrician slipped out his back door, drunk, looking for a spare bottle of bourbon in the garage. All those power lines snapping, all that work to be done. *One more drink*, he said, *just one more drink and then I'll sleep.* And he did sleep that night, in the emergency room with a bloody sock wrapped around his fist.

Grandmom chimes in that she was housebound under fifteen feet of New England snow that night, but no one listens. We're all tired of that story. But they insist on telling the one about me, the fourth Benjamin Kale, a boy born into an ice storm. They like to say how exciting that was. All this despite the fact that not a single one of them stood present for the event. Least of all my father. He'd gone turkey hunting. Which is to say he'd driven two hours north

1

of Mobile to the cabin in Barlo and gotten nasty drunk on Wild Turkey bourbon. His gun sat on the rack while he passed out in front of a dying fire. We used to own that cabin, not to mention the three thousand acres around it, but we've lost it all to the Lester family since then.

Now we tell stories about the old days, about times when the money held out, when it stretched far enough to keep up appearances, and about the little boy, a first born son who emerged glowing and beautiful in the midst of something as dark and dangerous as an ice storm.

I know. I'm drinking as I tell you this. And I imagine you'll want to know how I feel about it. So I'll tell you. I've already decided to tell you everything. Don't worry about that. And not the old romanticized stories of better days, but the real stories, the ones that actually mean something here and now. If I'm honest, the whole thing makes my stomach twist and keeps me up most nights. Nightmares, when I finally do sleep. Quite a bit of drinking too. I'm not proud of it. I may be the only one who hasn't glossed and polished our stories into something to be proud of, but like I said, I've already decided to tell you everything.

I'm doing this for you.

Just listen to me.

THE DOGS GO TOO

I'm sorry to tell you, sweet girl, but I might be a writer. I might be a writer who, on occasion, squirms into a tweed jacket and gives a quick reading. I might be a writer who goes to dinner parties and laughs loudest and can sometimes tell the difference between syrah and merlot (not really, but I'm full of bull). I might lift my glass into the light and I might sniff the cork. I might be a writer who will teach his students why plot does and does not matter; why character means more than anything; and why, if I'm honest, I don't care what they write about as long as they get a bang out of it and I don't get fired. I'm also in debt, drink too much, don't have health insurance, and ask strangers inappropriate questions on a regular basis. Lately, I'm thinking I should stop using the word *might*.

You should know, sweet girl, I might even be a writer with dogs.

Just last month I picked up an abandoned pile of wiggling mud from the middle of the street and took her home. I gave her a bath and let the vet fill her full of antibiotics. Now it seems I have a puppy who looks exactly like a raccoon had sex with a fox. She has a bandit's mask, a puffy cinnamon mane, and a black stripe that starts at the nape of her neck and ends at the tip of her tail. She has a white swirl on her chest and ears like a wolf. I named her Zuppa

3

for how much she looks like the espresso-and-mocha-soaked pound cake dessert we shared on our first night out. I named her Zuppa so that we would both be reminded of sitting across from one another and smiling wide when we realized how good espresso and mocha could be when it's soaked up by pound cake and topped with whipped cream. I also tasted spiced rum and amaretto, and when I watched you lick the whipped cream off your lips, it was the closest I've ever been to attaining enlightenment. It made me a little sorry that the man you were looking at was me.

Blue, a 13-year-old Border Collie mix, is my first love. Blue knows her left from right, the difference between the Packway Handle Band, Grass Town and Seldom Seen, and has convinced more than one female police officer to let me off with a warning. She is made happy by the sound of her own bark; embarrassed by her own farts; and if I am anxious and stressed, tells me she loves me with an empathetic barf. No one believes it, but Blue knows how to give me a wink if I say something worth listening to.

I have dogs and a pick-up, sweet girl. No sports car, no luxury sedan. Not even an eco-friendly hybrid or an electric or anything that runs on corn oil. And when I'm in my truck, it's blue jeans and bluegrass and baseball caps. It's sneaking cigarettes and a pint of scotch in the glove box. Sorry, sweet girl. When I'm in my truck, I can roll up my sleeves, keep a hammer on the floorboard, eat three cheeseburgers and drink all the full-strength Cokes I want.

But most important, when I'm in my truck I can bring my dogs. Real live dogs. Not the idea of a dog, and not some metaphorical construction. But the flesh and bone and bug-filled fur. Most of all, a soundly thumping heart. In the truck, I'm not some stuffy writer pretending to love dogs because he knows he's supposed to; I'm just a guy on the road with his mutts. Some guy with a sorry-looking beard and a pick-up truck and a crazy-eared half-human, half-canine stretching her head out the window, snapping at flies and anything else that might drift into range.

The thing about dogs, love, is that they change you. It can be a subtle thing, like a voice the person conjures when talking to a dog. A sudden shift from stodgy business lip to smoldering tones and indulgent cooing. Or it can be a full-body transformation. A lightning bolt through the nervous system that sets your Soggy Susan neighbor into jiggly fits of: *Who's a cute girl? Who's the cutest?* And: *That's okay! Your Auntie Susan doesn't mind a little mud on her skirt!* Don't fight it, sweet girl. They change you for the better.

The only place I go where they don't allow dogs is the library. It's worth it for the reading, but oh how it kills me. I know they are taking turns barfing on my bed and wondering just who I think I am, and I'll tell you, some days I'm not at all sure. It is at the library that a writer should really feel at ease. But not me. No, just a quick reading stop now and then, and that's about all I have the strength for. I need the dogs more than I need the books. That's for certain. I think I might enjoy playing the part of being a writer more than actually being one. So, sure, I go to the library, but if they would just allow dogs, well then, I'd be a changed man.

When I'm in my truck, it's a time machine. Blue jumps in and sits up like a person (because she is, dammit) on the front seat with her nose to the wind. Zuppa is still a puppy, so she curls into a sleepy ball on the floorboard, exhausted from her daily wrestling match with the neighbors' cat. And me, I'm traveling backward, full tilt to a time before all this writing. A time before all this man-made stress and man-made worry and no libraries! Right now I'm about 19, sneaking cigarettes, eating cheeseburgers, turning up the bluegrass, and all I can see is the Georgia blacktop ahead, the pine trees blipping past to my left, and to my right two very good dogs. Two very good friends. Blue takes a french fry with her talented tongue and sucks off the salt and spits out the potato. Zuppa barks at bicycle riders, and both, for about the hundredth time this month, make me ecstatic to be alive. It's dog-made happiness, and you can't beat it with all the fancy cars and fat salaries in the world.

I might be a writer, but I'm also a man with a truck and two dogs. I'm a man who gets in that truck and forgets about all the horseshit and remembers what his soul is made of. When I pull on a soft pair of beat-up jeans and roll up my sleeves, the person I want to be appears. No illusions. No metaphors. I am sitting right here in this truck. So when I show up at your house, don't be surprised that up in the front seat, sitting like a person (because she is, dammit), licking the salt off french-fries and spitting out the potato, is Blue, right here beside me. She always has been. In a few short months, Zuppa will be up to speed. But I've got a back seat and they'll make room. They know you're worth it. They know you'll come around.

I'll give up cheeseburgers and Cokes. I'll quit sneaking cigarettes and lay off the booze. I'll even trade in my pick-up for something that runs on corn oil as long as it plays bluegrass and has room for two big-hearted dogs. Two dogs and you. I'll do just about anything to see you lick whipped cream off your lips and smile wide across the table at a man like me. A man who might be a writer. A man who might be a writer who looks like me and who has two dogs who go wherever he goes (including one hypothetical library).

Please understand. Please don't fight it.

Because when I've finally convinced you to join me on this journey, when we've come to that happy middle ground where everyone gets enough of what they need and learns to let go of what they don't, and when you show me again that knock-out smile, and when I'm finally convinced that it is really meant for me, well, I'm sorry, my dear sweet girl, but the dogs go, too.

And maybe we'll get them into the library, one day. Or

maybe not. Maybe that's just going to be a part of our process. Let the dogs have time out, then get some reading and writing done. But you'll be allowed, sweet girl. They would never close a door on you.

CAT STORIES

There are dogs here. You know that by now. But there are cats too. Lurking at the edges of my story, stealing glances from a darkened room, sleeping in the sun-filled window, padding quiet paws from rug to rug in the dead of night. Our cat is obese. Twenty-five pounds and socking it away with no end in sight. Big Fat Frankie. Little Frankie as a kitten, but that was four years ago. These days his pin head is the only thing little about him. Pin-headed, pigeon-toed, knock-kneed, and a dangling belly rubbed bare from dragging the ground. But I need to tell you about the other cats first. We'll get to Frankie soon enough.

Camille and I drive from Mobile to Ocean Springs, Mississippi for Joel's baby shower. Conner and Joel. Conner is Camille's brother. Joel is his husband. Now, Alabama has changed over the last half century, but not so much that two men marry, in-vitro fertilize a surrogate mother, and throw themselves a baby shower without a flood of gossip washing across the Gulf Coast. On the way in, we pass a teenager dressed up like Jesus. He wears a crown of plastic thorns, fake blood, and a white sheet wrapped around his hips like a diaper. He carries an impossibly large wooden cross up and down the sidewalk. He shouts memorized biblical verses on the evils of homosexuality. But the boy is sweating and breathing so hard, shifting the cross from one shoulder to the other, that it's difficult to make out his words. In the time it takes us to move through the stop sign, he drops the cross twice. The blood on his feet is real.

A mile further we turn into the driveway, and I brake hard to avoid the overturned mailbox. The box itself had been beaten flat, and all but one pink balloon has been popped or cut loose. I move everything into the grass next to the garbage cans. Camille ties the balloon to the branch of a roadside azalea.

Inside the house, Dave Brubeck and shrill laughter lead us into the living room. Joel wears on his head a green blanket sewn in the shape of a tree frog while Conner takes his picture. *Screw the baby*, Joel says, *this is mine*. Joel's mother, Mary, laughs so hard her shoulders bounce and her eyes fill with tears. But she doesn't look at Joel. Instead, she looks to Molly. Her daughter sits Indian style on the floor nodding and gesturing, and egging on Joel. Molly purses her lips and croons, *Too, too gay, Mooky. Even for you*. Molly holds a kitten in her lap.

A year ago, we'd all come here for Mary's birthday party. Champagne fogged her etiquette and in short order she told us stories about Joel in his younger, wilder days. Stories filled with drugs and nudity and evading police. Stories explaining the nick-name Mooky. But she also told us her cat story. It's *her* story, I know. But I'll tell you just the same.

Mary used to live on an acre lot outside of town. The house was small and the land untamed. A tangle of vines and toppled trees created a crosshatch of thick underbrush. Hector, the cat, claimed the acre. Hector was one hundred percent Maine Coon. Big, muscular, and fast. He hunted at night, producing birds, snakes, moles, and mice by morning. One acre; no more, no less. Then Mary inherited her mother's house on the water and moved to Ocean Springs. The house is a beautiful old cottage dating back to the civil war. But the yard is small. A few feet of grass on one side, a few feet of sand on the other. Hector didn't seem to mind. Mary let him out at night and, as usual, he returned by morning. But it wasn't long before a neighbor warned Mary that her Tuxedo cat turned up dead. *Attacked by wild animals*, the neighbor said. Then another cat. And another. We drew a map of the neighbors' yards and property lines and stuck push pins into the crime scenes. One acre; no more, no less. Seven cats in all. Hector kept his acre under careful watch for three years. Then, without warning, he disappeared. Hector was fourteen years old, so Mary says he slipped out one night, beyond his claimed acre, to die an honorable death in private. I made a joke about Achilles, but I won't do it again.

Now there's a new cat: Galen. He's a foster kitten with a cold, blowing bubbles from his nose. Mary says: *He is Irish and he is lucky*. She brought him home last month when the doctors released Molly from the hospital. Galen is temporary, but it looks like Molly will stay. From the scar on her chin, you'd think she fell while skating or playing tennis or learning to sail. You wouldn't guess that a Mercedes smashed her Buick and sent her into six months of coma. You'd never know that only in these last four weeks, Molly has regained control of her mind. She's holding Galen and stroking his back. She's giving him another antibiotic for his cold. She's nuzzling his ears with her nose. Mary sits back and laughs, tears welling up and shoulders bobbing. You can see the release in her face. You can see the look of a woman who held her breath for seven months, until now, at this very moment, when a girl makes a joke with her words in the right order and smiles and strokes a kitten at the same time without forgetting who and where she is, and that the first breath is the deepest and most remarkable thing a mother can feel when a child is returned to her safely.

Joel takes the frog blanket off his head and passes it to Mary. She holds it with both hands. She grips it tight.

There are more cats.

When my father married his fourth and final wife, she brought two cats into his home. Houdini and Hegel. They were long and sleek and entirely silver. I couldn't tell them apart, and I'm not sure my father could either, but his wife would spot one in the shadows from across the hall and call out: *There's my little Dini. Why are you hiding? Come out and say hi to Mamma.* Houdini would stare for a moment more, then vanish into nothing. Hegel was more social, according to the wife, and liked to chase toys on a string. She also said Hegel and Houdini didn't get along at night, and that they could hear hissing and running at all hours.

I should warn you up front, this cat story ends badly. Hegel, the supposedly older cat, jumped onto Dad's bed at three in the morning. He tip-toed up the middle, between the two sleeping bodies, and then inexplicably jumped with all four feet onto Dad's chest. Dad woke suddenly. He was confused. He shoved Hegel off his chest and into the air. He searched frantically for his glasses, finding them just as his wife turned on a bedside lamp. Next to the bed, Hegel lay in the fetal position, dead. The vet said he was very old and the fright of the incident may have caused heart failure. *It's hard to say,* he said with open palms, *cats are mysterious.* The wife mourned Hegel for weeks, and it wasn't until Houdini took to sitting in Dad's lap that she forgave him.

Of course, this ends badly too. All my father's stories end badly.

It seems that some cats, in this case a sleek, silver cat named Houdini, are capable of sensing ailment before human or machine. In time, doctors would discover a tumor in Dad's liver. The tumor would expand and spread and turn his insides to rot. Just as you and I know this, Houdini knew it too. He would sit purring in Dad's lap, thinking about that tumor, and the next one, and trying to stay as warm and still and comforting as he could. When Houdini climbed up on the reading chair, he moved paw by paw, slow and deliberate and careful. He made sure Dad was watching before taking the step from leather to flesh. This was all he could think to do.

At the shower, we sit in a large circle and pass the gifts around for everyone to see. We also pass ultrasound photos from the surrogate mother, and baby pictures from those who have them. Camille digs into her purse and pulls out pictures of Big Fat Frankie. We have shots of him sitting, lying down, and eating. This is all he does. I've tried diets, but he squalls all night to be fed. If I put down fat-free cat food, he grunts and goes next door to the dog bowl. The food is far too big, but somehow he'll wedge a chunk of kibble into his teeth and shatter it. Then he moves methodically, eating all the pieces one by one off the kitchen floor. I even tried exercise. I filled a toy mouse with catnip, tied it to a string, and ran around the house with it dragging behind me. Camille has a picture of this too, but I've asked her not to show it. At first, Big Fat Frankie caught on to the game and lumbered after me. I have been told this lasted exactly fifteen seconds. Then, exhausted, he waddled up onto his bed for the three extra inches of vertical visibility and lay down. I made three more laps of the house with the dog barking and turning circles before I saw Camille grinning and taking pictures. Then I watched her feed Frankie goose liver pâté with a spoon. Right now, one picture going around the circle gets bigger laughs than the others. Joel holds it up for Molly to see, and she shows it to Galen. He blows bubbles with his nose. Camille grabs my hand and smiles.

"So who needs a cat?" Mary asks. "The vet called with a

new stray for me, and Galen needs a good home. He's done what he came here for."

Molly lowers her brow and makes a crease between her eyes. "What kind of cat does the vet have?"

Mary flushes red and says, "Maine Coon."

Molly stands and hands Galen to Camille. Then, as if planned, Mary and Molly break into a secret dance. They point index fingers skyward and twirl.

Camille drops Galen into my lap.

"We've got room for a skinny one. Right, Ben?"

On the way home, we crane our necks to see Jesus-boy on the sidewalk. He's propped the cross against a pine tree, and now free of his burden, sits quietly on a park bench. I suddenly realize I know him. I've seen the boy shucking oysters on weekends at Wintzell's. It's hard work and he's good at it. His hands move fast. I don't know his name, but I pull the car over anyway.

"Is the tirade over?" Camille asks. She's crossed her arms and looks down on the boy. "Is that enough hate for one day."

"Who cares," he says, not looking up. "My feet hurt."

"But there are so many more mailboxes in the world," she says.

Jesus says nothing. His chin shakes a little and his eyes go wet.

"Why are you doing this?" I ask. I sit down on the bench and place my hand against the cross. It's at least eight feet high. Camille tries to lift it, but can't. Her face changes and she turns back to the boy.

"My father calls this the sacred seamless garment," he says. "I look like a jackass."

"No way," Camille says. "Ditch the cross and the thorns and the blood and you look hot."

"It could be worse," I say. "The Roman's stripped

criminals nude for extra humiliation before a crucifixion. At least your Dad didn't know that."

"Extra humiliation?" he says. "I'm the one in homemade underwear."

In the late afternoon sun, Jesus-boy's curly hair lights up. His stomach is full of muscles and his ropey arms and legs turn bronze. If he could grow a beard, this Jesus would be perfect.

"Am I in trouble?" he asks.

"Let's make a deal," I say. "How are you with cats?"

Cats are not like dogs, and I won't pretend I don't have a preference. But I will say this: when a cat finally decides to make an appearance, when he finds the desire to communicate something to the one person who has been carefully chosen as the best equipped to fill his need, you can bet your life that you'll know what he is trying to tell you. The point will be perfectly clear.

ALABAMA

Heather was born in Alabama. So was I. This is something I like to say. In Alabama, shrimp and oysters taste a little like champagne, and the crab trap haul is fifteen pounds, pulled up hand over hand, the rope stained brown and slick with algae. Blue crabs snap three-inch claws in the air. I know how to reach around from behind and scoop them up without getting pinched. I know how to pick the white meat from the shell and throw out the dirty gills. They call them Dead Man's Fingers. Heather and I know these things. We were born here. I'm going to ask Heather to marry me, and I've got a ring in my pocket to prove it.

Another thing about Alabama: you can slip a kayak into Dog River at six in the morning and paddle out into Mobile Bay, passing under the concrete bridge, skirting the south side of the peninsula, and land on Goat Island for a rest before noon. I bring along a sandwich, and if no one is looking, I stash a six-pack of beer between the flares and emergency rope. Sea gulls flutter over the water before landing on the sandy beach. The gulls don't get many visitors, so they hop around and squawk as if you're not there. Heather likes to take her bathing suit off and lie naked in the sun. She does it without even grinning. I can hardly stand it.

We have parties on the water. Someone will make a few
calls and the whole mess of us shows up at the Bay with an
ice chest. We bring Mountain Dew, Mellow Yellow, Sprite,
and three bags of ice. We'll pour in two fifths of vodka,
two fifths of gin, and two fifths of grain alcohol. Our buddy
Sandman will mix it all together with a wooden paddle. He'll
stand on top of the ping-pong table and swing the paddle
over his head. His hips swivel and his butt sticks out. He'll
say, *Get Green! Get Green!* We'll shout and cheer. One cup of
Green is enough, but on a dare, we drink five. That same
night, David Letterman announces that we have the highest
teenage drinking rate in the country. He carts a keg out to
center stage and pours a beer from the tap. He raises the
plastic cup and says: *Mobile, Alabama, this Bud's for you!* We're
green to the gills when he says it, and the party erupts. We're
not sure, but we think we've won something.

Some parties, Heather and I sneak out the screen door
and make a quiet left onto the beach. Half the crowd is in
the house and half is out on the dock. We get 50 feet away
and take all our clothes off. We step out into the warm
coppery water, so still and smooth and shallow, and ease
under the neighbor's dock. We'll hide in the shadows and
watch the party. We reach up and grab hold of the low
support beams. We have acrobatic sex, half above, half
below the water, our bodies suspended and feet swirling
above the sandy bottom. When we return to the party,
Sandman points to our dripping hair and says, *Green and
Wet! Wet and Green!* Everyone knows where we've been. It's
like that in Alabama.

But later, in college, Sandman choked on his own vomit
at a frat party. His mother started an anti-hazing campaign.
They put his face on a billboard between Mobile and the
beach. We're not sure how to feel about it. The first time I
drove by, I cried. The next time, I punched the dashboard.
These days I just give Sandman a wave and think about him

swinging that paddle over his head. Heather will play with the radio when we get close. That, or she'll climb into the back seat for a Coke. Not everything in Alabama is like it used to be.

Another one of the gang, let's call him Polk, was walking downtown from one bar to another when a guy stopped and asked for money. Polk tried to give him a five-dollar bill. He took it out of his wallet and everything. But the guy pulled out a pistol and shot him. He still had the money in his hand when the ambulance found his body. Since Polk was white and the guy was black, the police decided it must have been a gang initiation. They said it happens that way. We don't know if that's true, and I don't imagine we ever will. Either way, we miss Polk real bad. Polk and Sandman both.

Heather's parents live down the street from mine. If I stand on Mom's balcony, I can hit Heather's house with a tennis ball. So sometimes I lob one over. When the ball hits her roof or mailbox or window, I feel that much more connected. Even if glass breaks, it's worth it.

When it snows in Mobile, the whole town shuts down. The joy of running out to the yard and rolling around in the first snowfall in seven years is like heated sex. Your face turns red and you can't feel your feet. And when you spot the kids across the street seeing snow for the first time in their lives, it's that much better.

Heather and I made a snowman in the field at the local college. When you've only got an inch to work with, you need as much surface area as you can find. The snowman turned out all brown and splotchy from the dirt on the ground. We used a cigar for a nose and a banana for the mouth. We didn't have buttons for eyes, so we used oyster shells from the driveway. We named him Santino. The kids who showed up loved him. They invented a dance and twirled around him like a maypole. Santino stood for three days. When the college kids got back from Christmas break, they made like pro wrestlers and body-slammed him flat.

All summer, thunderstorms march in like clockwork. Three o'clock in the afternoon and the sun disappears. The rumbling begins and the air tastes like you put a penny on your tongue. If you're lucky enough to be on the dock, you can climb in a hammock and watch the storm move across the Bay. Funnel clouds spin up from the water and lightning drops down fast and hard. By four o'clock they've packed up and gone. Mom is afraid of the storms. She was born in Montana.

But Mom is as much a part of my Alabama as anything. She made me learn to swim when I was three. There's a lot of water in Alabama. I was terrified. Coach Hanks picked me up and threw me in. I flailed my arms and kicked like crazy. *Look*, he said, *the boy is swimming now*. And I was. Ask anyone in Mobile how they learned to swim and this is what they'll say: *Coach Hanks picked me up and threw me in.*

Mom read that blueberries improve memory, so she stocked up. Four plastic containers a week. On cereal, on ice cream, in cobbler, plain, whatever. When I came home for Thanksgiving, I asked about it. Mom looked up from her cereal. *Don't you love them? Delicious!* Yes, I agreed, but why so many? *Well, I read something about them. Oh, I don't know. Eat up!*

That was after Mom locked the combination to her safe in her safe. She didn't realize what happened until she couldn't find her pearls. Then she couldn't open the safe. The locksmith laughed and said it happens all the time. *Really*, he said, *I get this everyday*. When it was open, Mom looked inside and couldn't find the pearls. For a week she argued with her husband about who lost them. About who stole them. About the cleaning lady, Rose, and the yard man, Moses. Then she noticed a false bottom inside the safe. Pearls. She went straight out and bought blueberries. Heather thinks this is the funniest story in the world. She asks me to tell it at parties. Heather's laugh is the Fourth of July to me. So I tell the story.

Right now I'm driving on Government Street and dropping down into the Bankhead Tunnel. I hold my breath. We all do. It's a ritual. You try to hold your breath until the car has made it underneath the Mobile River and come up on the other side. It started ages ago when locals noticed that car fumes collect in the tunnel. They say if you have an accident in the middle and try to walk out, you'll never make it. They say the carbon monoxide will kill you before you reach the end. They also like to scare first-timers by saying that if just one tile comes loose, if *just one tile* in the ceiling begins to leak, it will all come crashing down. It's a myth, of course, but we hold our breath just the same.

In the summer of 1941, Congressman Bankhead built and named the tunnel in honor of his daughter, the actress Tallulah Bankhead. She had just divorced and the gesture was intended to lift her spirits. The Congressman, so moved by love and pride, is said to have cried at the ribbon cutting.

All right. I'll admit that's not true. The tunnel was named after the drunkard Congressman by a circle of stiff-necked suits in the cold rain. Tallulah was busy making movies, sniffing cocaine, and recovering from advanced gonorrhea. She did not attend. Now don't you like my story better?

My cousin is also named Tallulah. She shares the name with her mother and grandmother and great grandmother. This is something we do. But when the youngest Tallulah names her first born daughter Anastasia, the adults hold their tongues. But not us kids. We smile big as moons.

I'm on my way to the eastern shore of Mobile Bay. That's where we have our parties on the water. It's also where we have a thing called a Jubilee. Only one other place in the world has them. It's somewhere in the Middle East. But here, when the moon and wind and tide are just right, the oxygen levels in the water change. The flounder and shrimp and crab come right up to the shore to breathe. At least, that's the theory. No one really knows for sure why it happens. But that's a jubilee. If you're out late at night and you see the shoreline dotted with crabs, cup your hands around your mouth and shout, *Jubilee!* Then we'll all know. We pull out gigs and nets and buckets and lanterns and get knee deep in the water. Sometimes the catch is so great we give it away.

Stingrays and catfish swim in the shallows too, and once I got a dorsal fin through the arch of my foot. It had to be surgically removed. But danger makes it more exciting. At least for me.

I read a story once called "Mississippi." The guy who wrote it says this: *Our crickets are trained to sing prettier and more convincing and purely than nature should allow. Mississippi is a special place. Some days I like to go out in the tall grass and roll around like a dog.*

So I say this: *Our crickets have not been trained; they perform by the power of instinct. When green tree frogs join in with the voice of bells, the music, so sweet in timbre, has been known to heal the sick. Alabama is more than special; it is mythic.*

Some days I like to jump headfirst into the Bay and swim the bottom like a catfish. I'm lean and fast. I was born here.

In Mississippi, gambling is legal so long as the building sits out over water. Biloxi and Tunica are famous for floating casinos. Gambling is illegal in Alabama, but in my lifetime we've elected a governor who never went to college. Now that's risk.

Mardi Gras started in Mobile, Alabama. This is something I like to say. *Mobile, in 1703. Not New Orleans. Go look it up.* Mardi Gras is like heated sex. Your face turns red and your feet go numb. When the kids come out to Bienville Square and see it for the first time, it's that much better. Parade floats in tongue-biting colors turn down St. Francis Street and costumed revelers throw candy and strings of beads at the crowd. You'll drop a bare knee into spit, spilled beer, and muddy gravel just to snatch up a Moon Pie worth less than a nickel. You'll risk your life diving between muscled bikers for the bigger, longer beads. The ones that almost look like something. You'll hoist them over your lover's head and say how sexy they look. Heather loves the beads. I leap above the crowd like Flipper and pick them from the air.

A secret society called the Mystics of Time puts on my favorite parade. They send serpentine dragons through the city streets. Masked men ride the dragon's back and smoke pours from its mouth. When the dragon stops in front of the square, we all jump up and down, waving our arms and shouting the names of masked men we think we might know. Heather likes to say they single her out. That of the hundreds of blurry faces in the square, a drunken man behind a sweaty mask throws a single string of beads, just for her. She doesn't even lift up her shirt, and I believe every word.

In Alabama, you can find clothes in the trees. I pulled a tweed sport jacket from a low limb of an old oak right in the middle of town. It was just hanging there. I put it on. It fit. Weeks later I found a dry-clean slip in the breast pocket. The name on it was Sherwood McBroom. I know him, of course. Alabama is like that. *Hey, Woody, I have your jacket. I'm wearing it now. Don't I look great?*

When I get to the Eastern Shore, I follow old 98 through a tunnel of oak trees. Then I'll make a right down Heather's driveway in a little town called Fairhope. It's her grandparents' house, a little white cottage on the red bluff overlooking the water. The story we tell about Fairhope goes like this: the first colonists took a look around and said, *This place has a fair hope of success.* There's no record to prove it, but we tell the story again and again. The Eastern Shore has their own Mardi Gras. We come over for a parade by the Knights of Ecor Rouge. A few years back, the parade was named *A Knight at the Movies.* Heather's father dressed up as Darth Vader and rode a float made to look like the Death Star. When I stopped to pick up Heather earlier that day, he answered the door in full costume. I was a little drunk. His costume included platform shoes. I said, *Don't hit me,* before realizing it was okay to laugh.

There are no parades today. This is summer. And when I get to the door, I look straight through the glass, down the hall, and out the back to where Heather sits on the sleeping porch. Instead of knocking, I ease around the side of the house and army crawl behind a row of azaleas. I pull the ring from my pocket and ready myself. Heather is less than 10 feet away. My hands shake. I watch her through the screen and think about all the years I've been coming here. I think about all that coppery water slapping the shoreline behind me. I think about Sandman and Polk and I wonder what they would say. I bet Sandman would make fun of me. I bet Polk would pretend not to cry. *Hey, fellas, I'm going to do it now. I'm going to marry that girl from Alabama. This isn't a dare. I'm really going to ask her.*

Just watch me.

SHACKLEFORD STREET

I f I'm honest, there's a stepfather in all this. His name is Virgil. Dr. Virgil Cross. He's a little Napoleon. A perfectionist. When we knew him, Virgil practiced neurosurgery at Saint Mary's. He was sued. I don't know what he does now, but I doubt it matters. The miserable tightwad penny-pinched millions. He's short, short-tempered, long-winded, and demands that his eggs and bacon are hot and ready at five a.m.

My mother married him when I was two. She divorced him when I was twelve. I left for summer camp, as usual, and a month later came back to a liberated home. That ugly brick rancher on Shackleford Street never seemed so big. I could walk up and down the hallway on my hands. My father paid for the house. Virgil just lived there.

Sometimes Virgil took me fishing. We drove over to Mississippi. Virgil's father had left him a trailer on a lake somewhere south of Hattiesburg. We put an aluminum Jon boat in the muddy water and fished. After a silent hour I didn't want to fish, of course, so I wedged my pole between the ice chest and the bait bucket. I leaned back and shot rubber bands into the trees. I always kept a pocket full of rubber bands. When one got stuck in the branches, I found it very satisfying. The others fell back down onto the lake and floated at the surface. I guess I'd shot a dozen when

Virgil popped me with the end of his pole. He didn't want
rubber bands in his lake. Maybe he didn't realize the hook
on his lure would cut me. The scar isn't a problem. I can
hide it with my bangs.

Then there was the time I stood at the edge of their
bedroom door, looking over the bed and into the bathroom.
I could see his naked back in the doorframe. He raised one
muscled arm with his small, red fingers gripping the scalpel.
In the mirror, I could see my mother. She stood with dark,
bleary eyes, arms extended and hands out. Her pink
nightgown seemed much too big for her body. He said: *I
know just where to put this.* Then he turned to leave. I dropped
out of sight and crawled to my room.

At twenty, my mother asked what I would do if I saw
him. It's remarkable that in all the years since the divorce, I
haven't seen him. Not then, not now. Not a single passing
glance in our little Alabama town. When she asked, I said:
I'd give him the bird. Everyone laughed. I think I laughed too.
But that's a lie.

If I saw him today, I'd look for something heavy. A
wrench, maybe. A lead pipe. I'd go after him without words
and swing that pipe. I'd go for the head. I'd see if I could
split the little general's skull and dash his brains.

If he's alive, that is. He was so old, even when they were
married. His close-cropped, ruddy hair turned gray and thick,
black bifocals clung to the end of his nose. I would think
he's dead by now. It's funny that I don't know.

I dream of that house on Shackleford Street most nights.
When I wake up sweating, having been chased and hunted,
my limbs in slow motion and the shadowy figure grabbing
at my feet, I wonder what it is I can't remember. When I
dream of the pitch-black room with the whispering voice,
that horrid low breathy voice whispering at me from the
darkness, I wonder what else might have happened there.

After Virgil left, we sold the house and moved to a cottage on the other side of town. I've never been back to Shackleford Street.

If I'm honest, I say this: *Look out, Virgil. If you're not dead yet, don't linger under streetlight. Don't hang around parking lots or pay phones. Keep to the shadows. If I see you, I'll split your skull. Believe me when I say this: my hatred is true.*

But sometimes I have another dream. The one where the ceiling has fallen out of my childhood bedroom and my mother demands to know why I did it? I tell her I didn't do it. *It just fell,* I say. At this point in the dream, she turns and asks me something else. *Did you do this because you resent something? Did you do this because you resent me?* And I shove her away and say, *it just fell, goddammit. It just fell.*

Then I wake up, sweating, and wonder what it is I can't remember.

THIS IS MARDI GRAS

We fly in first-class on Piggy Bank's dime, arriving at eight o'clock on Friday morning. The limousine driver with chestnut skin holds up a sign with our names on it. We drink single malt scotch from crystal glasses as New Orleans jaunts past through one-way windows. Tourists in T-shirts and cargo-pants try to see who we are. Let me tell you, they think we're famous. The scotch is Johnnie Walker Blue. Bartenders charge thirty dollars for a glass, neat, and I spill some in my lap. The driver, Sweet Comfort, reminds us that champagne brunch on the patio at *Bayona* will begin in two hours. He calls us *Mr. Husband* and *Miss Wife*. He's in full livery.

"Ya'll best take it easy now."

"We slept on the plane," I say.

"All right. All right. Just don't let it slide," Sweet Comfort says. "Mr. Piggy Bank wants everybody on time. He goin' all out."

Wife says, "So are we."

At the Wyndsor Court Hotel, we shower and change in deluxe accommodations. Our rooms have more square feet than your home. We have a foyer and mini-kitchen that bleeds into a den with three sofas. Beyond that, a dining table set for eight. Then a step through French doors reveals a king-sized bedroom with a king-size bed that opens onto a balcony overlooking the Mississippi River. If you press a button at bedside, a television rises up from inside an antique chest. We use perfumed soaps and tiny bottles of lotion. We drink beers from the mini bar and charge it to the room.

"It's too much," I say.

"Piggy Bank's got it," Wife says.

"I shouldn't have opened the scotch in the limo."

"That's what it's there for."

"Still. It was Blue."

"We're married. He's your brother too."

"I'm uncomfortable," I say.

"So take off your coat."

The limo arrives at ten o'clock sharp and shuttles us to *Bayona's* where Piggy Bank opens the first bottle of Dom Perignon with a sword. A smooth, white smile never leaves his thick ruddy face. Fifteen bottles are popped in all. The wait staff runs in and out and in and out and our flutes never go dry.

The rest of the party consists of Piggy Bank's wife, her divorced parents, her siblings and cousins. Don't forget Piggy Bank's family, the half-brothers and half-sisters and a menagerie of friends. All flown in first-class. All expenses paid.

This is New Orleans. This is Mardi Gras.

As we are seated, Piggy Bank's wife Silky clinks a silver spoon against her glass.

"It's time for Dirty Beads. You should all pick a number from the bag Sugar is carrying to your tables. Once you have your number, start thinking about which set of beads you want. Other Girl, show them the beads." Other Girl begins lifting beads from a bright green bag, one by one. She makes hand motions like Vanna White. She has the same hair. On the first set of beads, tiny lights blink inside translucent pink gambler's dice. Another has cartoonish boxes of Viagra and a life-size penis dangles from the bottom. Bald Guy tries to grab them, but Other Girl slaps his hand. One after the other, she goes through two dozen beads. The last ones, plastic oysters with black and white pearls, she holds over her head and twirls on a finger.

The rules of the game make no sense. Everyone is drunk. Piggy Bank snatches the numbers out of our hands and throws them on the ground. He stands on his chair and tosses beads across the room. He throws some over his shoulder without looking. I catch the blinking dice. Wife catches the oysters. Other Girl already has the penis beads hung around her neck and no one tries to take them.

"Sir," a waiter says. "Could you step down from the chair, please?"

"This is Mardi Gras," Piggy Bank says.

"Sir, we'd hate for you to fall."

Piggy Bank slips out a fifty and folds it into the waiter's breast pocket. He's still smiling. The waiter leaves the room.

The parade starts at noon. Piggy Bank owns a huge double-gallery style house in the garden district, directly on the parade route. White columns, black wrought-iron gate, and courtyard pool. He has an iron lion's head in the wall that spits a continuous stream of water into a fountain. His bedroom ceiling is painted in gold leaf with an oval mirror above the bed. Bald Guy calls it the Hotel Frenchafornia, but we all know his ex-wife Sugar said it first. Piggy Bank bought the house so we could watch the parades without driving or walking. He bought it so we could use the bathrooms and not the port-o-lets. He bought it despite the fact that he lives in Connecticut, works in New York, and only makes it down two weeks a year. Two weeks for Mardi Gras.

This is it.

In the middle of the crowd on the sidewalk, we've put

together a kitchen of crawfish and boiled potatoes. We've
got fresh silver queen corn and a half dozen king cakes.
We've got cases of beer and wine. We've got expensive
scotch. Piggy Bank stands in the middle of us in coat and
tie and sunglasses. He's red-faced and smiling and waving
to friends all over the street. Silky hands plates of food to
anyone within reach. A Stranger stops and taps my shoulder.

"Who is he?" A Stranger asks. "Is he famous?"

"Have you seen the movie *Wall Street*?"

"Yeah."

"He's Gordon Gecko," I say. Then I wink.

"So cool."

A Stranger kneels down and lifts a beer from the cooler.

"Cool?" she asks.

"Cool," I say. "This is Mardi Gras."

The floats cruise past, then the high school bands, then
the cops on horseback. Then the next float, the next band,
the next batch of cops. It goes on like this for hours. Bald
Guy throws his arms over Piggy Bank's shoulder and drinks
scotch from the bottle. He may be the father-in-law, but they're
exactly the same age. I eat a few crawfish, wipe the burn of
spice from my fingers, and chase it with beer. But I'm not
hungry. Wife catches a plastic headband with googley eyes
on springs. She puts it on and does an eighties dance routine.
I'll admit to you that she is good looking, very good looking,
and her neck is entirely hidden by beads. I snap a picture.

After the parade, Sweet Comfort drives us back to the hotel.

"*Port of Call* at eight sharp," he says. "I'll be right here at
a quarter of."

"What do we wear?" I ask.

"It's a burger bar, Mr. Husband. It don't matter."

We shower and change into casual clothes. I stretch out
on the bed. Wife stands on the balcony and watches people
milling in the street.

"Anyone naked?" I ask.

"Not anymore," Wife says. "A girl on the corner did a quick flash."

"How was it?"

"Very pale."

"How much do you think this room is a night?"

"She was sort of droopy."

"Six hundred?"

"What? She didn't even get beads."

In the lobby, we meet up with Sugar and Sage, Other Girl and Other Boy, and, of course, Bald Guy. He's still drunk and puts a hand on my shoulder. He holds up a digital camera but his hands shake and I can't see anything.

"Check this out dude," he says. "Kiss."

"Kiss what?"

"Gene Simmons, man."

"I'm good."

"No man, Gene Simmons." Bald Guy squints his eyes and sings, "I, wanna rock and roll all night, party every day."

"KISS," I say.

"Right here in our hotel."

I steady the camera and look at the tiny image. Bald Guy and Gene Simmons, arm in arm.

"Excellent," I say.

"He's riding tonight."

"Gene Simmons?"

"I'm gonna get hammered."

"Excellent."

You and Bald Guy wouldn't get along.

The limo picks us up and winds through back streets. We pull up from behind *Port of Call* and get out. Piggy Bank is already there, wearing a white linen suit. He's taking drink orders on the front steps and yelling them over his shoulder to the bar.

"I'll be right back," I say.

"What?" Wife asks. "Where?"

"Across the street. They've got a cash machine."

"What do you need cash for?"

"He's not buying this too," I say.

"Of course he is. But you can try."

When I get back, everyone is seated and drinking hurricanes.

"I got your hurricane," Piggy Bank says.

"That's okay," I say. "I'll get a beer."

"A beer?"

"Sure."

"Pussy."

No one pays any attention. The burgers and baskets of fries come, and I eat fast. I order a dozen boiled shrimp and eat that too. Crab cakes. Even the jalapeno poppers. I use extra horseradish in my sauce. When they take my drink order, I ask for Delirium Tremens. You know the one. It's the beer with a pink elephant on the label. I tell them to bring me two at a time. Then I ask for a dessert menu, and I'm told that all they have is chocolate cake. It's not what I want, but I ask for it anyway. By the time it comes out, it's time to go. We stand on the sidewalk while Piggy Bank pays the bill.

We make our way to Bourbon Street and join the crowd. It's like walking into a thicket. Six steps in and you disappear. I grab Wife's hand, but everyone else is gone. Just freaks in costume, men in drag, whores on the job, and pickpockets. We move deeper into the street and I make a fist around Wife's belt. Beads sail through the air. Men and boys, and sometimes girls, throw them at Wife. She smiles and says thank you. Sometimes she does a little curtsy. Then three women on a balcony above the souvenir shop lift up their shirts. Countless thick-necked meatheads gape. The crowd stops moving and we're trapped, bodies pressed together hard.

"I can't breath," Wife says.

"And they're ugly," I say.

"This is miserable."

"Let's try for that bar."

We push our way off the street and manage to cut inside a place called Fat Catz. It's less than standing room only, but it's better than outside. I pay cash for two Coronas and we sip them in the corner. Wife leans against the wall.

"This is better," she says.

"For now," I say. "We'll have to get out somehow."

"But this is better."

"Yes. This is better. But I'll want to get out soon."

I get bumped by the guy next to me and it's clear he's been shoved. He pulls a fist back and sets his jaw.

I say, "It's not worth it."

The guy looks at me. He holds his fist in the air.

"Bullocks," he says and throws the punch.

The cops arrive instantly. In less than four minutes, they break up the fight and haul three people to jail. That's the rule on Bourbon Street. If you fight, you go to jail. Get it off the street. Sort it out later. We watch it like a TV show.

When it's over, Wife and I take alleyways to Royal and make it back to the hotel by midnight. We're not tired yet so we walk upstairs to the Polo Lounge for another drink. Bald Guy is there with a glass of pink champagne in his hand. He's doing some sort of dance move and the girl he's standing with giggles. Her sequin skirt stops an inch below her crotch. Sometimes less.

"My buddy Gene and I rode with Endymion tonight," he says.

"Gene who?" she asks.

"I, wanna rock and roll all night."

"Gene Simmons?"

"Don't say it too loud," he says. "He doesn't want anyone to know he's here."

"In *this* hotel?"

Bald Guy winks and smiles. He orders another pink champagne. He charges it to Piggy Bank.

"Do we stay?" Wife asks.

"We've still got the ball tomorrow night. Commander's Palace on Sunday. I think there might be a lunch at Galatoire's."

"I don't have the endurance for this trip," she says.

"I don't have the clothes for this trip."

"Stop it."

"Let's head up then. Get some sleep," I say. "We could go for beignets in the morning?"

"Of course we'll get beignets," Wife says. "This is New Orleans."

"And it's Mardi Gras."

"That doesn't matter."

"Either way, I'm buying."

"You're so cool."

"You go ahead then," I say. "I'm going to step outside for some air."

"I forget, does air suck or blow?" Wife narrows her eyes. "Well. Take your time."

Wife turns on her heel and makes for the door.

We push through the weekend, overeating, overdrinking, overspending. We have trout almandine at Galatoire's. We have shrimp remoulade at Commander's. We have the finest champagne everywhere we go. In between, in limousines, we drink Blue. Piggy Bank never stops smiling and Bald Guy never gets sober. You would have never stopped laughing. And not just everyday laughing, but the kind where your eyes pinch shut and your hands shake. I could watch you laugh like that for the rest of my life.

But before it's all over and before we fly home, first-class on Piggy Bank's dime, this one thing happened that I haven't told you yet. I'm not sure if I should. We were in his double-gallery house. After the parade, but before Port of Call. No big deal. It's just another story.

We carried leftover parade food and booze into the house and picked at lukewarm crawfish. Wife napped on the couch while Sugar and Sage watched TV. Bald Guy drank scotch and twisted unintelligible words on his tongue. He took wobbly steps to the kitchen island. He grabbed on with both hands. Then he lifted his head and focused his eyes. He spoke, maybe to Sweet Comfort.

"You know that girl," he said.

"Which one?" Sweet Comfort asked.

"The one with google eyes." Bald Guy put index fingers on top of his head and wiggled them like antennae. His drinking voice boomed through the house.

"You mean Miss Wife."

He arched his back. "Came to see me last night. She's as tight as drum. Mouth like a Hoover."

Silence. No one moved. Not even me.

I was on the phone with you.

Piggy Bank stood near enough to grab Bald Guy's collar and drag him out of the room. It was over in seconds. A door slammed, but we could still hear the shouting. Silky asked if anyone wanted a drink. Maybe I should tell you that Piggy Bank is having an affair with a woman named Florida. Maybe I should tell you that Silky wants a divorce and that everyone is waiting to see who gets the house. Or maybe I should just tell you what happened next.

Sweet Comfort took a few steps over and squeezed my arm. He wore the penis beads over black livery.

"It's Mardi Gras," he said. "Folks act a fool."

I shrugged my shoulders.

"You should go back to the hotel," Wife said.

"I would like to clean up," I said.

"Come on then," Sweet Comfort said. "I'll take you home."

Mardi Gras parades move through the streets in a cloud of beads and Frisbees, embroidered panties and silk roses, a hail of plastic cups and silver coins. Every few years, someone will fall from their float and die. Some are crushed by the wheels, others by the hooves of horses. There are isolated incidents of stabbings and gunfire. But for the most part, the parades move smoothly. The girls who lift their shirts get the most loot. Little boys with fishing nets scoop up the rest. Everyone else taps feet and sips beer and smiles at how much dirty chaos one city can get away with. They fly in from all over the world. They buy souvenirs and expensive dinners and Johnny Walker Blue. They keep hotels in business. It's very carefully maintained. Men like Piggy Bank own this town. I pass through like a tossed stone, skipping across the surface of the Mississippi River for a brief moment, only to drop and sink beneath the muddy water. Just like Bald Guy. Wife is somewhere in between. Very soon, an epic convergence of hurricane swells and weak levees will change the city forever. But for these few seconds, the parade holds us together. As bright and blinking as an elaborate string of beads. Next year, let's go to Mobile Alabama, you and I. After all, that's where the entire affair got its start.

But here in New Orleans, we all reach up with waving hands and lifted shirts and fishing nets and hopeful eyes. We reach up to catch them. This is Mardi Gras. I've got a piece of it right here in my hands.

I Crossed My Arms
and Shook My Head

I'd hung half a ceiling of drywall by the time the radio announced the first plane collided with the North Tower. The contractor, Mack Mills, stomped into the house yelling, *Did you hear it, did you hear it?* And since Floyd listened to a little radio while he worked in the room above me, we had. There were sections around the fireplace where Floyd could hand me nails or a chalk line, straight through the floor, or ceiling, depending on your point of view. So, yes, we heard it. All of it. And I'd said, *It's the War of the World.* After I told Floyd what that meant, we both got a good laugh in. I held up one hand and said, *Martians land in New Jersey,* then held up the other and said, *Planes crash into The World Trade Center.* Neither one of us believed it was true.

Mack stood under the hole in the ceiling and said, *Got-damn got-damn! I think it's for real. They had it on another station in my pick-up.* Mack smelled of pot and beer. He was the first one on-site and I assumed he slept in his truck.

Despite the cold, I was sweating already and stripped out of my canvas jacket. I opened a Coke and leaned against a sawhorse, listening to the news. This may sound strange, but all I really thought about was the girl with almond skin. Floyd handed the radio down to Mack and ran around to the stairwell. By the time he made it into the room, they were saying a second plane had hit the South Tower. Reports of fires and explosions and men and women leaping to their deaths came in minute by minute. The girl with almond skin felt like electricity against my fingertips.

"I can't believe they got two of them," I said.

"Who's they?" Floyd asked.

"The people who crashed the planes," I said.

"Shit man, what the fuck do we know."

"With one crash, yeah. We know dick. But now they have two," I said.

"Still," Floyd said.

Now we stood in silence. Now I believed it was true. I couldn't help but think of our proximity to Washington D.C., a hundred miles at most, as we cowered around a little black radio in rural Virginia. The girl with almond skin lived in D.C. The radio reported a third plane. Now the Pentagon was on fire. I tried to make a map in my head of the Pentagon and the girl's apartment. It seemed as if you could throw a Frisbee from one to the other.

Mack Mills hitched up his pants under an enormous belly. He grabbed at his thick beard and stuck out his tongue.

"Times like this," he said. "I like to be home drinking and holding my gun."

"Fucked up," Floyd said. "Who knows what's next."

"D.C.," I said. "I'd bet they hit D.C. again. It's too good a target."

"And it ain't far from here," Floyd said.

"Fuckin ain't." Mack raised his brow and bugged out his eyes. "Fuckin ain't far at all."

"What do we do now?" I asked. I imagined driving to D.C. through a shower of crashing planes. I'd scoop up the girl with almond skin into my arms and run from the burning building. I'd carry her into the woods, laughing by the time we felt safe, and press our foreheads together, making grand, sweeping promises.

"Shit," Floyd said. "Work, I guess."

"Yep. We still got jobs," Mack said. "Turn that shit up so we can hear it while we work."

"So we're working," I said. I knew my wife would drive to the work site any minute now. She would say she was worried. She would use this to check in.

"Finish this ceiling," Mack said. "It ain't gonna drywall itself."

I was cold again, so I put my jacket on and started to work.

I sat with my wife in our little cabin, the fire in the woodstove and the coffeemaker spitting and popping as if in conversation. We sat on barstools at the butcher's block tabletop drinking wine with the dog curled up beneath us. A ring of pots and pans hung above our heads. The radio was off. I kept a bottle of scotch and a pistol under my socks.

The girl with almond skin worked at the capital for a southern Senator. She knew a man who was killed. By the end of the week, we all would. I went to see her on the 12th, taking the day off work, lying to my wife, and driving fast up 29 North. I felt electricity in my hands with every curve of the road. I looked up at a clear sky as I drove, nothing but birds breaking the blue.

The girl with almond skin opened her door and grabbed my waist, something like shock in her eyes, and held me tight. I couldn't think of anything to say, so I kissed her. I kissed her hard and slid a hand under her shirt.

"Is this what you want?" she asked.

"What do you want?"

"Everything." She put a hand on my belt.

"I want you now," I said.

"And later?"

"Later we'll go out for lunch. We'll pretend it isn't dangerous."

"After that?"

I pushed a black skirt off her hips and onto the floor.

Mack Mills stomped into the house, smelling of pot and beer, and hitched up his pants.

"Finish the fucking ceiling," he said.

"I'm almost there," I said. "I'll mud it, sand it, paint it."

"He got here early," Floyd said. "Way before me."

"Makin' up is good, but not missin' in the first place is better."

"I'm working hard," I said. "I'm getting it right."

"Is that why I see gaps around the electric plugs and chimney?"

"I can fill it with mud."

"Not that wide." Mack put a finger between the drywall and socket. "You mud this and it'll crack and fall out. Do it again."

I crossed my arms and shook my head.

My wife kept the cabin but I kept the dog. Mack Mills threw a bucket of wet cement at my head, so I quit. The girl with almond skin married the Senator's son and took up in a perfectly restored, silver-shingled Colonial on Martha's Vineyard. I sent her a letter of congratulations. I even think I meant it.

This may sound strange, but I smiled all the way out of Virginia. I drove south with all I owned in a trailer behind me, a blue sky marked by crossing planes, gliding smooth and fast to intended destinations. I passed into Tennessee, still smiling, and waved at a pretty girl sitting on a bench in front of a truck-stop diner. She looked up, seemed to know me, and reached her hand skyward with every finger outstretched. She waved as I drove. Between us, a field of heather seemed not to know the season.

Fire engine red, it bloomed.

WHITE BOY

The gunshot sends me running. I pump my arms and make up the spread by the end of the first turn. The inside lane is my favorite. I'm faster when I reel them in. This is the local meet at our rival's track: Midtown Prep. We're all white here. My school, Springhill, is coed. Midtown is all demerits and paddles and takes only boys. Other than that, we're the same. Rich, private, and white. My great grandfather built Midtown's auditorium, Kale Hall, in memory of my grandfather. He was killed by Japanese kamikazes. I've seen pictures of him before the war, running on this very track. His sister says that when she watches me run, she can't tell the difference. She says running genes must skip a generation. I pass under the shadow of Kale Hall at the top of the second turn. We hate Midtown. They hate us. My quads burn by the time I hit the straightaway and lengthen my stride. Four hundred and forty yards.

This is my race. So I win it.

Coach Volks jogs over holding a stopwatch an inch from his nose.

"Great race, son." He clicks a button with his thumb. He holds a hand over the face to cut the glare and shows me. "Fifty point seven."

I'm bent over, hands on knees and huffing my breaths.

"Next time," I say.

The four-forty is excruciating. I'm not trying to sound melodramatic; the race is hard. With sprints, you never run out of air. With distance, you work yourself into a rhythm and look for the fastest pace your heart can sustain. The four-forty is different. It's everything you've got for a quarter mile. One lap around the track. Your muscles run out of oxygen at the final turn and it's a mental battle from then on. You can see the finish line. You know it's almost over. But the knives start in on your quads, the pins drive into your knees. Fires burn under your feet. The last stretch hurts worse than a fist fight. You have to believe you can't feel a thing.

I'm trying to run it in under fifty seconds. This isn't a record. The 6A kids break fifty every time. But we're a small school in a small division in Mobile, Alabama. I'm the best we've got.

The next meet is County. Then it's State. The rumor is that our division, 4A, will be combined with 5A at State. It's still not 6A; that would be murder. But we're scared just the same. The public schools find bigger and stronger runners. They're all black. Some of them even have beards.

Dad calls and says he wants to go hunting in Barlo. He slurs his words. Not all of them, but enough to let me know what I'm in for.

"Let's go this weekend," he says. "Opening weekend."

"Really? Opening weekend?" I ask. "Yes!"

"Sir."

"What?"

"Yes sir."

"Yes Sir. Wait. I have County meet."

"What's that?"

"I have to be there," I say. I sit on Mom's bed. I curl the cord between my fingers. "The team. We've been training."

"This is a matter of priorities. What's more important to you, running or family?"

"They need me to run the four-forty."

"Is that a gun? I've got the 30-30 ready for you."

"That's my race."

Dad sighs. "Okay, next weekend. We'll miss the first shot, but the second weekend isn't all bad."

"That's the State championship."

"Jesus H. Christ." Dad emphasizes the 'H.' He slurs the 't' out of Christ.

"That's the most important one."

"Oh. I see. Then we'll go hunting this weekend and you'll do the run thing next weekend. It's opening weekend."

"But this weekend is County."

"Fucking A. Now if you can't go next weekend, and that's *the most important one*, then you're going hunting this weekend with me."

"Coach Volks isn't going to un-"

"I don't give a shit what Coach Polks thinks. He sounds like a vodka pisser."

Volks, I think. I pull my fingers free and curl them back into the cord. "What about the next week. After State?"

"Three weeks into the season?"

"But we could still-"

"It's settled. Four o'clock on Friday."

I want to say no, but work the phone cord instead. Dad hangs up. I listen to the dead line.

In his office, Coach Volks taps pen against clipboard. On the wall behind him, a plaque is engraved with his State Championship titles. He holds the national record for most consecutive 4A high school wins. *Sports Illustrated* ran an article on his career. Volks is bald, tan, tall, and strong. Some afternoons, he runs with us. I've never seen him drink.

"Where are your priorities? Is hunting more important than running?"

"I hardly ever see my Dad."

"Right. I get that. But when you make a commitment to the team, we expect you to be here every time. Are you a part of this team?"

"Yes sir. I am. I'm just, well, it's Dad. He's got this thing about opening weekend."

"I don't give a damn about opening weekend. But if you desert us at County, I'm not sure we should plan on you for State. We've got to mix it up with 5A boys, and they mean business. I don't want to slot you in for the big race and then get a no-show. Are you a part of this team?"

I sit still. I grip the edges of my chair seat and try to breathe evenly. I stare down at my legs.

"Look son, just see if you can get a run in while you're out there." Volks rubs his hands, palm down, on the surface of his desk. "You're a point scorer." He pulls a sheet of graph paper from a pile and points to my name in the left column. "We're counting on your points. Without you, we could end up eight or ten points down when it really counts. That could mean first or second in the state. Just look at the numbers."

I look at the paper, at the tiny boxes and pencil marks, and I understand more than I want to.

It's five thirty. Mom called Dad, but he's not home. *Must be on his way*, she says. I nod. We've made this exchange a hundred times. I'm wearing a new camouflage t-shirt from the Army-Navy Surplus outlet. Mom bought it. *You look like a little soldier*, she says. I made her buy face paint too, but I'm saving that for the woods.

For now, I grab my pellet gun and coat and wander into the neighbor's yard. We live in the old part of the neighborhood. The houses sit on plots four and five times bigger than the new ones. There's still a chunk of woods behind my neighbor's house, and I wonder how long it will last. I spot a squirrel at the base of a pine sixty yards away. I take a pot shot and miss. The squirrel scrambles up into the branches and clings to the bark. As I circle the pine, he claws his way around the trunk so the tree is always between us. I pick up a pine cone and toss it into an azalea beyond the tree. The squirrel moves away from the cone and into view. I pop him between the shoulder blades. He falls limp into the grass.

I run to the squirrel and grab him by the tail. I take him into my back yard and skin him out with my Swiss Army knife. The meat is so little, so delicate, I ruin most of it with the knife. I look back to our house, then to the neighbors. I bury everything behind the shed. I stomp the loose dirt until it's flush with the ground. Then I cover it with pine straw and go back inside. I put the gun in the corner of my closet behind a box of trophies and shut the door.

Dad turns into the drive at six fifteen. He pulls himself out of the Mercedes. He stands, keeping a hand on the car for balance, and finishes his cigarette. The sun is beginning to set behind him and the edges of his silhouette glow. I spot him from the window and go to open the door. Dad steps into the house slowly. He smells of smoke and cough drops and bourbon. We don't hug, but the smell is strong. Mom stands behind me.

"How's my house?" he asks. "Taking care of it?"

"The house is fine," Mom says.

"The yard looks shabby," he says. "Can't get those monkeys to do it right?"

"Honestly, the yard is fine," Mom says. "When will you have him back?"

"Should be Sunday afternoon. We might hunt the morning."

Dad's eyes are blood red. He pulls a cigarette from the pack in his chest pocket. He pops it in his mouth, wiggling it up and down with his lips.

"Please be. Please be careful," Mom says. She grips my shoulders hard.

"You bet." Dad lights his cigarette. "All right Ben, let's hit it."

We walk out onto the drive and Mom stands on the porch. I can see her breath. She puts a hand in front of her eyes to block the glare of a low sun.

In the car, Dad smokes and sips a pint of bourbon in a brown paper bag. The radio is on, but the volume is so low I can't tell what's playing.

"So Ben," Dad exhales. "How's school?"

"Fine." I hold my breath as we shave past a clump of mailboxes.

"All A's," I say.

"My eyes are killing me." Dad leans his head back and squeezes eye drops onto his cheeks and brow. A drop or two find his eyes as the Mercedes floats into the middle of the road. We straddle the dotted line.

"I'll just keep her centered," he says.

"Should I drive?"

"I've got it." Dad says this as if chewing on rocks. Then, "How old are you?"

"Fifteen."

"Got a license?"

"Learner's permit."

"Now why the hell didn't you speak up sooner?"

We pull over at *Papagayo's Stop and Snack*. Dad goes in for beer and cigarettes while I adjust the driver's seat. I can see okay, but the controls are different from Mom's Buick. I get the headlights on just as Dad gets back in.

"Let's hit it," he says.

I pull out onto Highway 43. Everyone calls it *Bloody 43*

for the accidents. City drivers in hatchbacks forget that loaded logging trucks can't brake on a dime. Once I saw a Honda pinned to a telephone pole. The rear tail light had been pushed through to the driver's seat.

Dad cracks a beer. "Good timing, too. It's nothing but dry counties from here on out. Juan is selling beer hand over fist in there. It's a goddamn goldmine for a wetback."

I drive ahead. Pine and oak trees blip in and out of the headlights. Pick-ups fly past in the left lane. I'm not sure about the speed limit, so I hold tight at 50. Dad finishes his beer and throws the can out the window. He opens another. I grip the steering wheel, leaning forward and looking for our turn. I'm hoping I'll find the cabin without having to ask. I'm hoping Dad will be conscious when we get there. I'm mad as hell at Mom for letting me go. I'm wishing to God I was home in my room, gone to bed early, and dreaming of my race.

Turning off 43, I find the Tombigbee River Bridge. On the other side, I take a right onto the red clay roads. These roads, so red in daylight it surprises me, turn the color of blood in moonlight. They wind through thick woods and pine stands, nameless, and I make turns based on a dip in the road, a license plate nailed to a tree, and the weedy cemetery. The gravestones here have faces on them called death masks. Mount Erebus church still does it. The reverend makes a plaster mold of the face before the burial, then fills it with concrete and tears away the shell. He mounts the likeness into the gravestone. The older ones turn dark and slick. It makes them look real.

Dad's been out twenty minutes. I drive slowly through the black night. A dogwood branch scrapes the side of the car and I snap my head to the window, eyes wide. All this darkness creeps into the car, shadowing Dad's face. He looks dead. I can't see his chest rise, but I can still smell his breath. I keep control of the car, making subtle turns to dodge ruts and holes. Then I change my mind and aim for them. Dad doesn't budge. When I find the cabin, I hit the brakes hard. Dad jerks forward, slumps back, and finally wakes. He looks over at me, dreamy eyed and confused. He sits up and purses his lips as if to ask a question. Then he stops. He turns and looks through the window at the cabin, nods, and gets out of the car.

The morning hunt comes and goes without us. Dad sleeps on the couch. I'm on the dock. The sun burns off an early mist and ducks gather, flecking the edges of a little island mid-lake. Baby alligators sun themselves on the sandy mound in front of their underground den. They make a throaty burping sound like no other animal. The mother is fourteen feet long and her head is as wide as my shoulders. I can't see her now, but with all these babies, I know she's close.

My great grandfather, the first Benjamin Kale, dammed the swamp and created this lake fifty years ago. He built the cabin and cut deer fields from the wilderness. He brought friends and businessmen up to this land on weekends, hunting the swamp in morning and the fields in late afternoon. He stocked the lake with bass and bluegill and fished the off season. The land sprawls out five thousand acres, winding alongside the Tombigbee and spreading out to higher ground in the east. We own just about all of Barlo. Except for the church and a cluster of black families near the road. They have squatter's rights. Dad calls them *cousins*. *The cousins got here before Granddad; we can't get 'em off.* Dad says this with a heavy southern accent. I've heard it a hundred times. His mother raised him in New England with her family after the war. Dad went to Harvard. He didn't return to the South until he was thirty. No one knows why he talks this way.

Dad gets up for lunch. I make tuna fish on Wonder Bread.

"Where should we hunt the afternoon?" I ask.

"I thought we'd try out the new shooting house by the barn."

"Have you seen deer in there?"

"Bucks move around. You never know." Dad sips instant coffee and smokes. Two bites of tuna and he's done.

I go to the bathroom and put my camouflage t-shirt on over long johns. It's too cold, but I want to wear it. I pull out the face paint and rub my fingers across the glazed surface. It's like shoe polish. It goes on smooth and I'm covered in no time. I had wanted to paint a real camouflage mask with greens and browns, but mom would only buy one tin. I picked dark olive.

When I come out, Dad gags on his beer. He laughs hard.

"Black face? Dressin' up like a cousin for the deer?"

"I'm camouflage," I say. My face goes hot under the paint.

"Jesus H. Christ." Dad emphasizes the 'H.' "How the hell am I supposed to look at you?"

We walk from the cabin to the barn in silence. From the barn, there's a thin trail through the trees to the shooting house. We climb the ladder one at a time, pulling rifles off our shoulders at the top and scooting sideways through the plywood door. I thought we should unload before climbing, but there is no discussion of safety. Inside, we sit in shadows at either end of a six foot bench. We face forward through a cut-out window draped in green cheese cloth, overlooking the field. Dad sips from his flask. He glances over and grins.

The gun in my hands is a 1932 Winchester 30-30 in mint condition. This is my first time to carry it. My grandfather's gun. The story is that he used it to kill a ten point buck in the swamp. They say he heaved the deer over his shoulders and hiked it right up to the skinning shed. Two miles through the mud with 210 pounds on his back. There are dozens of stories about Granddad. Dad says the stories keep his father perfect. *By the time you're my age*, he says, *they'll be making movies and comic books. Son of a bitch will be wearing a cape.* Dad was one year old when Granddad was killed. He carries a Remington 7mm with a fiberglass stock.

After an hour, does trickle into the edges of the field. They feed on grass, listening for strange sounds by flicking their ears side to side while they chew. I study their movements. One doe raises her head to look around, then another. They alternate the watch. As a new deer enters the field, the others freeze. They stare in the direction of the newcomer, waiting to be sure. They stamp a foot or give a low snort. Sometimes they flick tails up, flagging to the others with bright white fur. I think it's a buck every single time. My heart rate rises and my hands sweat. Dad leans his head back against plywood and closes his eyes. He cradles the flask between his legs.

"Why did you send me to Springhill, not Midtown?" I ask.

"Midtown is boys only. I worried you'd turn out a fairy."

"But the theater has our name on it."

"That's not my fault."

When the sun dips below the tree line, it becomes easier to imagine antlers. Every deer seems to carry a burden of horns. I lift the rifle and ease the barrel through a slit in the cheese cloth. I sight the deer in. Then, of course, she turns her head and the branches behind her stay put. I do this every five minutes. Dad's out. Thirty doe feed in the field. When another enters, I lift the gun.

This time, the antlers are real. I sight him in and count the tines. Ten points. My hands go clammy and my fingers tingle. I kick Dad's leg. He nods forward and squints.

"Hot damn," he whispers. "Shoot."

I'm shaking enough that I can't place the cross hairs on his shoulder. The buck keeps moving, sniffing the air and nosing the ground. When he looks to the doe, he grunts. He's walking across the middle of the field. It's only fifty yards.

"Shoot already for Christ's sake." Dad turns the last two words into one. "Come on, let's hit it."

He puts down the flask and lifts his gun into his lap. The buck lowers his head to feed. I hold my breath, but even then, I can't steady the gun.

"It's time," Dad says. "Shoooot."

I'm deaf with heart beats by the time I squeeze the trigger. The earsplitting report echoes off the plywood walls, but I don't hear it. The recoil bruises my shoulder, but I don't feel it. I'm shaking and sweating and trying to spot the buck. He's running fast, bounding yards at a time with all four hooves off the ground. I know I'm supposed to shoot again, but I freeze. The rifle has some kind of lever action, and I don't know how it works.

I jerk my head up when Dad fires on the buck. Tears and face paint fill my mouth. I look out on the darkening field. The buck lies dead in the corner.

We climb out of the shooting house and walk across the grass. A humid, fecund odor fills my lungs. I can already see the bloated white stomach rising from the ground. It looks so unnatural, so out of place, that I almost convince myself that when I get there it won't be real.

The buck's tongue lolls out, caked in dirt and already drawing flies. His eyes remain open, even as Dad nudges a leg with his boot. The antlers are perfect. Ten evenly spaced tines, bowing out, then curling back in.

We walk back to the cabin by flashlight. At the porch, Dad holds out a length of rope.

"Get back out there and tie this to the antlers," he says. "Drag his ass to the skinning shed."

I take the rope. Dad doesn't offer the flashlight, so I find my way by the moon. I'm cold. I find the buck, tie the rope, and start dragging. First I face the deer and pull backwards off my heels. Then I throw the rope over my shoulder and dig in with my toes. I switch back and forth. It takes two hours to drag the buck to the shed. When I get there, Dad stands with two black men. I recognize the bearded one from our last trip. They all drink beers. They're laughing hard.

"Hey, hey. Look who made it for dinner," Dad says. "Clifford and T thought we should check up on you. But I knew you could do it. First-deer adrenaline, I said. Ain't that right T?"

"That's right Mister Kale," T says. He scratches his thick black beard. "First deer and all."

I don't know the joke yet, so I stay quiet. I'm cold, thirsty, and soaked in sweat.

"Hey, Ben. A beer for you. It's your first buck." Dad hands me a can of beer, and not knowing what else to do, I take it. My hands ache with cramps and cold. My legs burn. The beer is bitter, but I gulp it fast.

"Look at him," T says. "Drinks like his paw."

"All right," Dad says. "Get this deer up on hooks and skin him out."

"Yes sir, Mister Kale." T grabs a curl of steel, like a giant fishhook, and pops it between tendon and bone, six inches above the back left hoof. He wraps both hands around the shaft and lifts the entire deer. Even with two thick shirts on, T's biceps swell visibly. He fits the steel circle at the end of the hook over a bolt in the frame of the porch. The buck hangs upside down. Blood gathers on the cement.

Dad hands me another beer. He pats my back.

"You know what comes next."

"Yes sir."

"Don't call me sir," he says.

"Yeah."

Dad takes a knife from his belt and slices the deer's hide. He cuts from crotch to neck, exposing guts and stomach. T pushes a tin garbage can under the belly and scoops everything out. When the stomach falls, it catches the lip of the can and tears open. A caustic stench hits us. I step back, but Dad grabs my arm.

"Oh no you don't."

Dad pulls me in close. He slides a bare hand inside the buck and brings it back bloody. He rubs his hand across my face. The smell is unbearable. He reaches in for fresh blood and slaps my forehead. The blood mixes with face paint and tightens my skin as it dries. Some of it gets in my eye and my lids stick when I blink. Clifford and T go about cleaning the buck.

"Now, I might be wrong, but I'd swear I heard *two* shots over here." Clifford points at a bullet hole in the front shoulder and smiles wide. "But I just see this one hole."

I step from the concrete into a patch of grass and vomit.

"Look who can't hold his liquor," Dad says. He turns from me to Clifford. "The kid missed the first shot, but he nailed the second one. Quick hands."

I'm on my knees, freezing. My legs twitch as I stand up. "I'm cold," I say. "I'm going in."

"You're a man now," T says. The men raise their beers while Dad lights a cigarette.

When I get to the cabin, I sit on the steps and unlace my boots. I look back to the shed as I pull them off. Dad unfolds bills from his wallet and hands them to Clifford and T. Dad points to his cooler and says to pack the tenderloins in block ice. He tells them to keep the rest. They open another round of beers and laugh about something I can't hear. Soon, Clifford and T will finish the deer and take the remains to the swamp. They will dump the guts, bones, and hide onto the pile. In less than an hour, the hogs and vultures will scavenge what's left.

I go inside, undress, and look in the mirror. My face is unrecognizable. I stand under a hot shower. Blood and face paint color the water pooling at my feet. When the water turns cold, I get out.

I dress, button up my letter jacket, and silently vow to never wear camouflage again. I steal a beer from the fridge and ease past Dad, passed out on the couch. An obscure station on the radio plays Robert Johnson's *Cross Road Blues*. I step outside and walk out on the dock. The purple sky is heavy with stars. Crickets and tree frogs sing at the water's edge, but I can't hear the alligators. I listen for their throaty call, but it's not there. When I finish the beer, I stand up and piss into the lake for what seems like forever. I go back inside, hoping to sleep. I'll dream of herds of sprinting deer. In my dream, they'll do nothing but run.

But now, stepping back into the cabin, Dad is awake and drinking bourbon. I can tell by the look in his eye, he has something to say.

"Hey hey," he says. "Look here you little shit. When are you gonna start acting white?"

Dad stands and bumps his drink with a knee. I take a step back.

"Gonna run off like a young cousin," he says. "Better head for the other cousins. Maybe they'll bow down to our new, great white hunter."

Coach Volks drives the team to Bankhead Coliseum for the Indoor State Championship. Curved buttresses extend from the oval dome to the black parking lot like legs. Everyone calls the coliseum *the roach*. In its belly, a crew of men constructs a wooden track with banked sides. They fit the pieces together as if it were an elaborate jigsaw puzzle. The outside lane rises eight feet above ground on turns. The best thing about the track is the sound. When a flight of runners rounds the turn, six pair of spiked shoes pound the elevated boards. The thunderous rhythm echoes like drum songs, rolling out from the track a half step behind their feet.

In the stands, Coach Volks hands out numbers and safety pins. He announces the order of events, time to allow for warm-ups, and foods he thinks we should or should not eat. *Keep hydrated,* he says, *keep loose but keep alert.* We stretch and jog in the outer hall. We peer into Midtown's section and wave to the kids we know. The Coliseum fills with strange faces and our hatred for Midtown wanes. We convince them to move down and sit next to us.

Mom sits with the other parents. She cheers for all of us by name. She underlines my race times in the program and shouts out when I need to be ready. Coach enters me in high jump, long jump, triple jump, and the four-forty. I do well enough in the other events, but all I care about is the four-forty. It's my race.

I win my heat of the prelims, but the time is off: fifty-one two. I'm slated to the inside lane for the finals. Coach Volks tells me not to worry: *You're faster when you reel them in.* But the roster makes me nervous. The top time is forty-nine seven. His name is Tyson. I don't know him, but I know he's 5A. I know he's black. I don't have any black friends and I'll admit that they scare me. They stand taller and stronger with arms and legs like steel cables. I'm rail thin with a mouth full of braces. My chin is as pink and smooth as the skin on baby mice.

Mom hands me Gatorade from the ice chest. It's cold and sweet. I gulp it fast.

"It's time," Coach Volks says.

"I'm ready," I say.

"It's time," Mom says.

"I know. I'm ready." I lace and double knot my spikes.

"Do you need a banana?" Mom asks.

"I'm ready," I say.

The finalists collect mid-track and I discover they're not all black. We have two white runners, two black runners, and me. The bigger black boy trots to each of us, nodding and shaking hands. *Good luck*, he says. *Have a good race*. He's got a thick, black beard and the brightest smile I've ever seen. This must be Tyson. His handshake feels like leather gloves.

I move to my starting line, yards behind the rest on the inside lane. I shake the nerves from my hands and bounce on my toes, stretching my calves and quads. When the starter calls us to *take our marks*, I put my left foot out front, leaning forward and balancing my weight with a hand on my knee. I throw my right arm back and suspend it mid-air.

The gunshot sends me running. I close the gap on the boy in the second lane by the start of the first turn. Tyson is in the third lane. His calves pop up and down like pistons. I catch the runner in the fourth lane as we curl out of the turn. The red line across the track signals us to break from our lanes and shift to the inside. I stay put, edging ahead of the boy from lane six. I move into second place. A group of girls with braided hair lean out from the first row of seats screaming, *Tyson, Tyson, white boy's coming!*

By the start of the second turn, I'm on his heels. I stay in his shadow until the straight. I move out into the second lane and drive my legs. Mom claps her hands and screams my name and I love her for it. Coach Volks smacks a hand against his clipboard and stands up in his seat. He calls out, *You've got it son!* The girls with braided hair chant, *white boy's gonna win, white boy's gonna win.* I lean forward and pump my arms. I drive my legs. As I pass Tyson, I move into something beyond pain, something out-of-body and dreamlike.

Soon, I'll stop running. Mom will scream my name so loud that it brings tears to my eyes. Coach Volks will show me his watch and I'll have crossed the line at forty-nine five. He'll tell me that first place brings ten points. That we've won the championship. He'll put his arm around my shoulder and squeeze. Even the guys at Midtown will applaud. When they gather in Kale Hall at school next week, they'll make the connection. They'll know where I come from.

Soon, we'll load up the van and start the drive home. When we reach Springhill, Coach Volks will be smiling when he says: *son, you know what comes next.* I'll nod and say *yes sir* as they grab me by the arm and throw me into the pool. My legs will go limp and I'll turn nauseous. But when the team shouts my name, it will be worth all that cold.

Soon, a crew of men will begin tearing down the wooden track. An expert will inspect the beams and battens, the tongue and groove, and judge the construction unsafe. They will remove the sections one by one. They will throw them all away.

But right now, I've still got fifty yards. Ten points are in my hands, and I intend to keep them. Tyson draws up on my left, but I find it in me and give more. I'm running harder and faster than I ever have. I lean so far forward I have to catch myself, but I don't lose my stride. Tyson recedes from the corner of my eye. His black beard is the last thing I see before turning numb. My head slips into a cottony haze. I can hear my spikes hitting the track like a fist pounding. The recoil of each footfall twists in my stomach. They hit so hard I'm shocked by the sound. But I can't feel it. Not the burn in my spikes, not the knives in my quads, not the pins in my knees. I can't feel any pain. I'm floating to the finish.

This is my race, of course.

So I win it.

THAW

I drive through an ice storm across Richmond, trying to make the Christmas Eve flight to Mobile. Icicles cluster in trees along the roadside, overloading them with unnatural weight and causing some to pop and fall. I chew gum and focus my eyes on the road. At the airport, they will only say that the flight is delayed.

"How long?" I ask.

"We don't control the weather," they say.

"This is Christmas."

"We know that."

I sit in a blue plastic chair for an hour waiting on updates. There are none. Then I wander the food court and newsstands for two hours. I buy three packs of gum and a copy of *Architectural Digest*. The feature article is a tour of Sting's English manor. At least one of his two Irish Wolfhounds makes it into every photograph. In the last picture, the hound named Finbar wears a red woolen scarf. When I return to the gate, the monitors blink from *Delayed* to *Canceled*. I reschedule for Christmas morning and drive home, chewing gum through a tunnel of exploding trees.

In front of my apartment, I look over my shoulder to the neighbors. I know Audrey has been gone for days, but I can't stop myself from knocking. No one answers, of course, yet I stand there for more than a minute. I let my forehead nod down and press against the cold wood before turning around to unlock my door.

In the kitchen, I unwrap one of a half-dozen frozen ribeyes my brother sent me for my birthday. I drop it into hot water to thaw, but it floats, so I pin it down with a butcher's block. I pour a scotch and water and dial my mother's number.

"I'm iced in," I say.

"How long?" she asks.

"I don't control the weather."

"This is Christmas."

"I know that."

After hanging up, I check on the ribeye. It has turned light brown at the edges and when I slit open the plastic wrapper, a smell like unwashed feet rises to my nose. I sip my drink and tap my boot against dirty linoleum. I look back in the freezer. Five left. I pull one out and drop it in the water. I pin it down. I take the rotten steak to the balcony and throw it in the direction of the apartment dumpster. I miss by thirty yards. The scotch has turned my gum hard, so I throw it out too. The parking lot is mostly deserted, but the gum is small and it is impossible to see where it lands.

An hour later, I check on the steak. It looks mostly the same with light brown edges, but I also note small patches of cloudy white. I slit open the plastic. This ribeye smells less like unwashed feet and more like baitfish left overlong in the sun. I step out on the balcony and hurl it across the lot. I miss the dumpster again but manage to hit the only parked car in sight. The thud is loud, much louder than expected, so I jump back inside.

I open the freezer. Four left. I drop one in hot water. I pin it down.

I pour another scotch and dial my father's number. His wife answers.

"Hello," she says. I cup my hand over the receiver.

"Hello," she says again.

"Ho, Ho, Ho," I say. "Have you been naughty or nice?" My hand still covers the receiver and she can't hear me.

"Is that you, sweetheart?" she says. "Come home, baby. I miss you too much."

She begins sobbing so I hang up. I finish the drink and unwrap a stick of gum. I hold it between my fingers for a moment, tapping my boot against linoleum, then drop it to the counter. In the upper cabinet, I find my cigarettes.

The next ribeye has the same light brown edges and the same cloudy white, but I also note a sooty dark spot between the flesh and the fat. I decide this one smells exactly like the crawlspace under my childhood home after my stepfather laid out twenty-five rat traps. I take it to the balcony. I light a cigarette, inhale deeply, and chuck the rotten meat with everything I've got. It lands on the roof of the mailbox hut, causing icicles to fall and shatter on the cement sidewalk. I find this very satisfying. I return to the kitchen and pull all of the remaining ribeyes from the freezer. I skip the hot water. Instead, I line them up on the balcony railing. One by one I throw them. They are hard and dense and sail through the purple sky. One hits the playground slide with a resonant thump and another bounces across the pavement, skittering into darkness.

In the morning, I'll drive back to the airport under a bright round sun, chewing gum as icicles melt away from surviving trees. I'll board the airplane and drum my fingers and chew as if chewing could make everything right. I'll land in Mobile and spend what is left of Christmas Day with my family. At one house, there will be a tree with white lights and presents tied in looping red bows. At another house, there will not. Before leaving, my mother will tell me that thawing meat in hot water is unsafe, and I will tell my brother that *they tasted just fine.*

But right now I am only able to focus my attention on what is directly in front of me. It's the very last ribeye arcing up and out, spiraling tight and smooth and fast. And finally, after an impossibly long flight, I focus on how it disappears, soundless, into an airy pillow of snow.

THE BLACK OYSTER

I step into the Black Oyster. Cigarette smoke hangs in the stale, bone-dry air. Barstools creak beneath a handful of heavyset regulars. A blanket of dust covers the pool table and the jukebox sits unplugged. Photocopied pictures of missing children hang by thumbtacks on the wall next to the door. I read the names—*Rhonda Spencer, Cindy Oates, Bart Wiseman, Holly Dorn*—and my stomach turns. My leather shoes stick to the floor as I make for the bar. I wear a white oxford button-down and beige chino slacks. The regulars sit with raised elbows in T-shirts and studded leather. An old sign behind the bar reads: *Great Service Deserves a Great Tip!* I take a stool at the nearest end while the bartender eyes me. My neck is tight and I massage it with one hand. It's only mid-afternoon, but I'm already drunk.

"A Glenfiddich, neat."

"Say again."

"Glenfiddich, scotch."

"We ain't got Glen-anything, pal."

"Talisker?"

"Nope."

"Dewar's. Surely you have Dewar's."

"No."

"Well. What do you have?"

"White Horse."

"All right. White Horse."

The bartender pours my drink and snaps it down dead center on a crisp square napkin. He looks to an over-muscled, middle-aged white man with a wide forehead and ZZ Top beard. The bartender methodically refills his beer mug without spills. The foam rises a quarter inch above the rim.

"You want a Glen-itch?"

"Nah, Charley, I already got one Glen-itch. I don't need another."

Charley laughs in a way I've heard serial killers laugh on the Biography channel.

"You've never heard of Glenfiddich?"

I ask the question sincerely enough, but even drunk, I know what I'm getting into. Everyone stares.

"What about Johnnie Walker Blue?"

The regulars look to ZZ Top and wait. I swallow my scotch.

"No, I ain't familiar with it. Is it any good?"

"Well, yes. It's better than White Horse. And I don't know what you've got for rail scotch, but I know it's much better than that."

Charley's hands disappear under the bar. ZZ Top shakes his head. Charley steps back and quickly wipes the oak with an immaculate towel. Trapezius muscles rise from under his black T-shirt and bulge around his neck like twisted rope. ZZ Top picks up his mug with three thick fingers. His pinkie knuckle is a knot of scar tissue. The finger is gone. He grinds out his cigarette, walks over, and takes a stool next to me.

"What the hell are you doing here?"

ZZ Top is at least six-four and smells like the inside of a bait well. His tattooed bicep is the size of my thigh.

"I'm having a White Horse, neat."

"You're looking to get killed."

"Something like that."

"Look smart-ass, get the hell out of here before I beat you like a dog."

I finish the glass of scotch here in the bar, but I'm somewhere else with Heather. We sit in her grandfather's house overlooking Mobile Bay, the house her great grandfather built between wars. Rain comes down in sheets and the surface of the water is impossible to see. It looks like static. Heather pulls her thick twist of hair back tight. Her green eyes distend with tears. *I'm not trying again*, she says. *I won't.* I hold my head in my hands. The wine bottle between us sits empty. A cigarette butt floats in her glass. *It's dead*, she says. *There's nothing else to talk about.* She makes for the door. I know I should stop her, but I don't. I sit there. Here at the bar. There on the floor.

"White Horse, neat," I say.

"Ok, you had your chance." ZZ Top steps back to his stool and drains a beer. Next to him, a short, bald albino man coughs and wheezes into a crimson red bandanna. He wears a black leather vest so tight that the seam arches between buttons. He sips what looks like milk from a beer mug. Charley brings my scotch and smiles as he thumps the glass down on the bar. Fresh napkin, dead center.

"That'll be... everything."

"What?"

ZZ Top and the albino laugh hard. The albino's laugh squeaks like a girl and his pallid cheeks turn pink. The dog collar around his neck flashes with chrome spikes.

"Everything in your wallet, that's your bill."

"What if I don't have anything in my wallet?"

Charley leans in so close I can see each red vein crawling in his eyes.

"Then we'll have to make other arrangements."

Charley's hand emerges from under the bar with a black billy club. The club is two feet long, slick with polish, and the words *Kill Stick* have been professionally engraved across the shaft. He stands stone-faced with the club in his hands while I produce my wallet. Charley's eyes, dark and recessed in his skull, do not blink. I shuck four twenties and lay them on the bar.

"That's what I've got."

Charley takes the cash and shoves it in his pocket.

"Now get out."

"For eighty dollars, I think I'll sit and finish my drink."

The albino calls out a childish, "Ooooooh." He clutches the bandana at his face. ZZ Top sighs in disbelief. Charley outweighs me by seventy pounds. His hands attempt to wring water from the club.

"I don't think you understand. Get out, now."

I take another deep swallow of scotch. I'm in her empty house. The Alabama sun mops the bay windows in orange afternoon light. Heather is here, reading. Her skin and hair seem to turn gold. She reads until the sun hangs just above the water and then slinks outside to sit on the fishing dock. I'm walking out to join her. I wish I could join her.

But Heather isn't really here, of course. She hasn't been for a year. One year exactly. Heather is in Virginia. As we speak, she's taking the Steele's Tavern exit through a cut of tall swaying pines, turning right at Steadman's Grill and following the winding black asphalt into the Saint Mary's wilderness. The orange sun clings to the needled treetops. She parks in the dirt circle and takes off her shoes. The ground is cold, but soft enough, and she finds the trail by memory.

Gurgling river-babble drifts in from somewhere beyond the trail and she picks her way through the brush to the water's edge. Slivers of light reflect off the water in curling arcs. The eddies swirl in violets and pink. Heather traveled here with her father as a girl. She collected flowers while he fished. Her favorite, bigleaf magnolia blossoms, are rare in these woods, but she finds an early bloom on a low branch.

She thumbs the white petals. She removes her clothes and eases down into the bitter cold. This time of year, the river swells with melted snow. She lies face up, watching the light shrink away from the tree tops while she sings, humming and crooning her mother's favorite Lightnin' Hopkins tune: *Long gone, like a turkey through the corn. Long gone, with my long pajamas on. Whoa look a yonder, whoa I see. That red-eyed captain, he's comin' after me.* She digs her heels in against a boulder, knees up, and holds herself in place against the rushing current. Her voice shudders in the cold, her fingers lost among the slick, moss-covered stones. Heather sings until she no longer feels her body. She sings until her empty body floats up and out of the water, rising into cirrus and stars.

The club hits my left eye, instantly swelling it shut. I fall backward and land on my tailbone. I hear something pop deep inside me. My head swarms with angry bees and a vision appears. Heather's hair, Charley's eyes, and the muscles of ZZ Top assemble into an imagined monster, beating me savagely. I imagine the sound of Heather making love, soft and delicate moans and gasps. The fall knocks the wind from me and I'm sucking for air. I roll over. From the floor, I see that more pictures of missing children cover the back wall. There must be over a hundred faces. ZZ Top lifts me by the crook of my arm and drags me to the door. With my head lolling forward, I glimpse blood on my shirt. The albino opens the door, waving *bye-bye* with his bandana, and ZZ Top throws me out.

I struggle to see with my good eye on the drive home and I can barely turn my neck. This house, the house my grandfather built for my mother, overlooks the Childress River. I head straight for the bathroom. Pain radiates from my tailbone. My eye is a perfectly round bulb of purple-black swelling. Some sort of ooze has leaked from the socket and the entire darkened area shines with glaze.

I shower, drape on a robe, and walk to the kitchen for

another drink. The bottle on the counter lies empty. In the cabinet, behind the vodka, I find a bottle of Glenfiddich and grin. I break the seal and fill a glass. The last of the afternoon light slants through the bay windows and I rush out the back door to join Heather on the pier. She sits perfectly still, golden in the setting sunlight with loose strands of fiery hair flitting at her shoulders. She holds a book in her hand, something called *Dog Fight*, and keeps her place among the pages with a finger. Heather wears a white cotton top with thin straps, and beneath, her black bathing suit clings to her skin. But this isn't summer; it's mid April. I'm about to ask about the bathing suit when I notice that she looks very much like a photograph I shot years before. I sit down, and as the bay swallows the sun, I realize this *is* the photo. From the black bathing suit to faint crow's feet at Heather's eyes, every detail of the photograph sits before me. Heather doesn't smile. She squints, but doesn't blink. I reach out with one hand to touch her. The sun dips beneath the horizon, the light changes, and Heather disappears.

I return to the house charged with energy. I pour another drink and pad toward the bedroom. My heart pumps in my throat and I incorporate dance steps into my walk. By the time I get there, I've begun to dance in earnest. I twist, spin, and give the bedpost a kiss. I throw off the robe and rifle through my hanging clothes. Nothing strikes me, so I run to the hall and jerk down the attic steps with a string. The steps unfold in the manner and sound of a tuneless accordion. I turn my head and climb into the darkness good eye forward. At the top, I pull a second string and flood the attic with light. I step a few paces forward to a gray metal rack. Formal dresses, costumes, and unworn winter coats hang from the rack in clear dry-cleaner bags. I pull a strapless black dress from its bag and dance into the Civic Center Grand Ballroom. Heather and I foxtrot on polished marble and I nod hello to friends and family. The Ballroom is dotted with debutantes, encircled by white-haired patrons, and rings of society ladies loop gossip from one end to the other. A forty-something redhead in an emerald sequin gown whispers to a platinum-blonde in purple velvet, *You've had your eyes done. They look wonderful.* She sips gin and tonic while the blonde nods up and down. The blonde attempts an exaggerated wink, but her face contorts into something vaguely painful.

The King of Mardi Gras steps carefully through the crowd. When he smiles, his eyes close. He grabs Heather's ass, then mine. The King looks as if every drop of blood in his entire body has risen to fill his puffy head. I turn back to Heather. She laughs, pointing to a drunken Knight's leg and boot emerging from beneath a dinner table. I laugh too, but stop when I realize I'm falling. Hitting, and then falling again. I could swear I hear an accordion play. The dresses and costumes fall with me, and I find myself lying on the floor of the hall, naked in a heap of regal attire.

Despite my now throbbing back and burning knee, I pick a set of white-tie tails from the pile and clamor to get them on. I also manage to retrieve an eye patch from an old pirate costume and gingerly cover my swollen eye. I take a deep swallow of scotch and soldier myself into the living room. Heather giggles and flicks on the stereo. The house fills with Leadbelly. I dance with Heather again, but this time we're alone. She smells of southern magnolia. We listen to her old blues recordings, drink scotch, and dance barefoot on a hand-woven Persian. The rug was a wedding gift from her father. Rich colors jump up to dance with us, swirling and rolling like waves. I begin to spin and ask Heather to help me. I grab for her, striking out with my hands in the air. I can't see anything clearly. Only flashes of hair catching gold light from the corner of my eye. The spinning quickens and the colors leap up to meet me, burning the right side of my face. I cry out over furious guitar rifts and raspy crooning, but Heather is gone.

I awake face down on the living room floor next to Leadbelly. He thumbs out a ballad, humming softly. I stand up, find my drink, and pour another. It is fully dark outside, and when I turn to face the bay windows, I can't see the river. I can only see my reflection in the glass. The eye patch has slid up and off my rug-burned face. The elastic string now pulls my hair into a violent, twisting crown. I raise my drink to the window and toast the new me.

Midnight at the Black Oyster. The regulars have not moved. They stare like wolves as I limp to a stool. By now, every inch of wall space is covered with missing children. In places, they overlap three deep. Some hang from the ceiling. Hundreds of shy little boys and girls watch my every move. The albino sucks down his milk by turning up the glass with both hands. He wipes his mouth with the bandana and coughs. His pudgy upturned nose runs beneath watery green eyes.

I hunch over and release two bulging paper bags from under my arms. Charley reaches for the club, but ZZ Top speaks up.

"What's in the bags?"

"Glenfiddich and Johnnie Walker Blue. Help yourself."

I pull a half dozen bottles from the bags and pass them down the bar. I keep the last bottle and ask Charley for three glasses. He plays along, producing the tumblers. He lays them out side by side on evenly spaced, clean white napkins. I pour scotch for myself, Charley, and ZZ Top. The albino keeps both hands wrapped around his milk.

"This is top shelf, gentlemen."

"There ain't a single goddamn gentleman in here."

"I disagree."

"This bastard is crazy. Do you know that?"

"All I know is pain and scotch."

To my surprise, ZZ Top lifts his glass in a silent toast,

and swallows down his scotch. The rest of the bar, including Charley and the albino, do the same. I watch the group toast through a mirror behind the bar. Standing in disheveled formal wear with a blackened eye and rug-burned face, I join a circle of wild men.

On the other side of the room, Heather sits in a booth with a small child. They wear glittered party hats and hold balloons. Heather is cutting a slice from a birthday cake when she catches my eye. She stops and blows me a kiss. I relax my shoulders and neck. And I stay relaxed, even as I see Charley sliding out *Kill Stick* in the mirror. The albino hides behind his stool, but he's not watching us. He's watching the birthday party. Charley assumes a well-rehearsed fighting stance and ZZ Top cocks back with an empty bottle. But even now, even as ZZ Top takes a swing, I smile. I've come to the Black Oyster for something awful, and the service is great.

POST-WAR HEAT

Slick with sweat, Sweets stops at the cargo train tracks to catch his breath and fan himself with the *Mobile Press Register*. He shuffles under the welded arch of the main entrance to the Alabama Dry Docks and a uniformed guard directs him to the employment office. Sweets already knows the way. He carefully chooses a path through piles of rusting scrap and crosses long, dark shadows cast by cranes. Sweets repeats his qualifications aloud over swollen lips. Near the dock, he stops in front of the tug boat, Little Ben, and catches his breath. The tug glistens with fresh paint and hand-rubbed teak. The owner of the shipyard, Benjamin Kale, tags his dead son's name to everything he builds. Sweets removes his hat and grips it to his chest.

"Hey now, look at ole Sweets," Wishbone shouts. "Goin' again!"

Wishbone is lean and tall with hair cropped close. He holds up his welding mask with one hand. His black torso swells with muscle.

The other men look up. They clap and whistle at Sweets from a cracked oil tanker prop. Wishbone drops his mask and relights the acetylene. A cloud of sparks, soot, and steam rises from his torch, then vanishes into white-hot sky.

Sweets resumes walking, eyes focused forward. At the

backdoor of the office, he tucks in his faded blue work shirt and mops his face with a rag. Inside, unemployed men work the maze, trying their luck at each glass window. Sweets rubs the foot of a rooster between finger and thumb in his pocket. He slows his breathing to even, controlled breaths, then opens the door.

Hours later, Sweets emerges from the building. He sits on the first step. His hips and knees burn. He struggles to breath. Sweets enters and exits by the back door every Monday. The other applicants sit out front. Among them, a young man with smooth almond skin slaps his thigh. He says: *No parades, no bond rallies, no jobs. Can't even shuck oysters.* The others nod. Some say, *amen.*

At the back door, Sweets looks up to Wishbone, blackened with soot. He sits down beside him. Both men drip with sweat.

"I'll get over to Dauphin Street," Sweets says.

"Kazoola's might need you."

"Sho might."

"Ain't no way to tell," Wishbone says.

"Got damn," Sweets says. "Maybe they'll be havin another war."

Benjamin Kale sits behind an ornate mahogany desk in suit and tie. He swivels in his chair and watches Sweets and Wishbone through the third-story window. He watches Wishbone move, shirtless, and presses his palm against the glass. Wishbone says something, gesturing with his hands, and Sweets nods. Cold air blows through newly installed air vents. From this distance, Wishbone could be any man. He could be white. He is young and strong and virile. He might be a navy boy, home on leave. Sweets might be his father.

Suddenly, the air feels over cold and Benjamin closes the vent. He opens the window and leans out as far as he can. He closes his eyes. On the desk, a black and white photograph of his son lies face down against the wood. In the picture, Ben Jr. sleeps on a riverboat bunk, his arms crossed behind his head. In another picture, still upright, twin baby boys peek out from under blankets in a bassinet. Ben Jr.'s wife will take them away. She will take them to her family in New England. They will be raised without a southern accent. They will not know that Benjamin hired Sweets to drive his polished black car, despite the slide in revenue. They will not know that Wishbone will use Sweets to break into the Kale family home.

What they will know is this: A man known as Wishbone split Benjamin Kale's skull with a fire iron and only got away with his gold watch on a chain. He was never found. My father will discover the watch in a pawn shop thirty years later. In thirty more years, he will die, and I will find it in his desk. I've got it in my right hand, right now. My name is Ben. It does not keep time.

1946 at the shipyard, Benjamin grips the window sill and inhales deeply. The hot air rushes in. He leans forward, so far forward he jerks, nearly falling. Benjamin never opens his eyes. He does his best to absorb the summer heat.

In the Attic

T he thing you should understand first is that the man from Tucson doesn't love me and I don't love him. So when he showed up on my Alabama doorstep with a suitcase and a bottle of wine, Husband thought everything was just fine. They shook hands and grabbed each other by the shoulder. You see, the man from Tucson—who became the man in our attic on a folding cot—was friends with Husband before everything happened. They met four times a week at the local gym and worked out. They spotted each other. That was before the night that I kissed him and before the night he invited me into his bed. They were friends and we were friends and I was married, but it all sorted out just fine. Now, however, while Husband cooks lasagna, the man in our attic seems to think we'll have another go, right here in our home.

The first night goes something like this: Husband makes lasagna with three kinds of cheese and the man in our attic, let's call him Tucson, has his hand on my knee under the table and it's headed north. All very predictable, all very clichéd. Until Tucson says to Husband, "What do you say we leave this pretty lady for a spell and you and I go out for a man's drink? A glass of single malt, neat, and a good cigar?"

And Husband says, "You're on."

So I'm home alone and not a clue what Tucson is up to.

You should remember that I don't love him and he doesn't love me so it doesn't matter, but when the phone rings I jump a mile.

"Hello," I say.

"On the cot in the attic, there's a picture of you coming out of the shower with the biggest grin."

"You kept it."

"I like to see you that way."

"Grinning or naked?"

"Wet."

I say nothing.

"I also have a pistol. A simple six shooter. Anyone could learn how to use it."

"We don't keep guns in the house."

"That's smart," he says.

Then Tucson hangs up. I was never sure if Husband wanted to go out or if he was just being polite or if he already knew everything and had other plans altogether. Between the two of them, Husband could always lift heavier weight.

Both men show up safely at midnight. Drunk, but otherwise unharmed. Husband won't tell me what they talked about but keeps making pistols with his hands and saying *draw!* followed by the imitated sounds of gunfire.

That was the first night.

On the second night, after sleeping late, and after a painfully silent lunch, Tucson suggests we smoke a little grass, and Husband—of all people—agrees. Now I don't know much about pot or getting high, but I went to college and learned a few things, so I know right off that what we're smoking isn't plain old marijuana.

Within an hour I fall into a blinding fog and can't be sure whose hands are under my shirt. It seems like Husband, and I sort of recognize his voice. Then I feel a third hand, and a fourth hand, so I fight for the wherewithal to push people away. But those hands keep grabbing and my skirt won't stay down, so I kick somebody hard in the balls. That's enough to get some distance and I climb the stairs into the attic. I pull the string for the light and there it is, perfectly exposed on the cot next to my dripping wet breasts and stupid grin. I pick it up. I didn't expect it to be so heavy, so dangerous. I guess I don't know what I expected, but it frightens me and I put it down. The breath on the back of my neck stops me from turning around.

"Do you love me?" the voice asks.

"Who are you?"

"Does it matter?"

And in that moment I guess it doesn't, because we climb into the cot and make the rafters shake. In the morning, I wake up alone in the attic. Husband can't remember anything, but noisily complains that his balls ache. As for Tucson, he and his pistol vanish. No note, no naked picture. Nothing.

So when you come to visit us, we'll put you up in the little study off the kitchen and it'll be just fine. I upgraded to a trundle bed and threw the cot away.

We no longer use the attic.

A WOLF IN VIRGINIA

H ere stands the wolf. This is surprising, as Seth lives in Virginia and wolves do not. But here he is, with a silvery back, dark shoulders, and eyes like water beneath ice. Seth's dog, a black and tan shepherd mix named Mingus, growls through the screen door. They look the same size, eighty, maybe ninety pounds. Devon gave the dog to Seth on his last birthday. Mingus still lives here, though Devon does not. The wolf sniffs the air and looks in Seth's direction. He wants to believe that some ancient migrational instinct has brought the wolf here. That, perhaps, genetic information from another era has inexplicably overridden the wolf's better judgment and delivered him, thin and confused, to these woods in Free Union, Virginia.

But this is not true, and Seth knows it. This wolf is from eastern Russia. He and his pack were shot with tranquilizer darts, crated, and set upon an ocean crossing cargo ship bound for the Chesapeake Bay. From there, the wolves were placed in temporary holding crates until Dr. Jacob Conrad, the head of the Wildlife Ecology Lab in Wisconsin, could pick them up. He recently resurrected the program after a lack of funding, and his own mental breakdown, closed the doors. The charges held against him for marking his territory in the university sculpture garden were dropped. Dr. Conrad planned to drive the wolves home to Wisconsin. There, he envisioned a spectacular release. In his mind, this project would both fortify the small population of timber wolves already inhabiting the region and restore his fading reputation. No one called him Wolfman anymore.

Elvis Moon had a better idea. Elvis lives about a mile down Miner's Mountain Road from Seth and works for the Virginia Department of Transportation; they all call it V-dot. It's not that Elvis loves wolves; it's that he hates beavers. Beavers are plentiful in Free Union. They cut down trees with their long, sharp teeth, as beavers tend to do, and as a result, dam rivers and flood roads. As a V-dot employee, Elvis is responsible for cleaning up the mess. Initially, V-dot encouraged residents to hunt and trap beavers. Elvis shot and killed 39 beavers himself. But not enough locals cared one way or the other; their oversized SUVs plowed through the two or three inches of flood water without ever slowing down.

Left to his own devices, Elvis would never have come up with his plan for the wolves. In fact, the whole thing started with Seth. He had been researching timber wolves for a magazine article on animal species recovery. Seth ran across Dr. Conrad's papers on the internet, phoned, and spoke to him on the subject of integrating new wolf packs into an existing ecosystem. Conrad held high hopes for introducing Russian wolves to Wisconsin. He said adding new blood to the genetic pool could make all the difference.

"Hell, have you been to the pound?" Conrad asked. "Those mutts have twice the health and vigor of most purebreds."

"My girlfriend picked up our dog at the pound," Seth said. "Mingus is the happiest dog I've ever known."

"But health. Not happiness. Health is what I'm getting at." Conrad paused and made a sound like he was smoking a cigar. "With all those combinations of genetic material, nature is able to build a better machine. No inbred mutations. Perfect chromosomal alignment."

Seth's father sits in his leather reading chair, bony legs cocked out, his right hand rubbing his swollen stomach. Seth's brother and sister-in-law stare at him.

"The tumors are pressing against my other organs," he says.

Linda holds her own swollen belly. "I think I know what you mean."

Henry tells their father that he loves him. He asks if there is anything he can do. He grips his knees.

The father stares out at the darkening bay through the glass door. "I don't know what in the hell anybody expects me to say."

Seth stands, slides open the door, and steps out onto the balcony. The redeye into Alabama left him with a sore back, so he lifts his arms over his head and stretches. A tugboat pulls a barge of coal along the intracoastal waterway. He tries to read the name on the tug, but it's too far, and the light is dim. Henry has followed Seth out and leans against the wooden rail.

"I guess that's all we can do," he says.

"I guess," Seth says.

"I mean, what would you say?"

"I don't know. Something. I think I would say *something.*"

"He's been drinking," Henry says.

"Of course he has."

"Where's Fran?"

"I couldn't get through."

"That's Fran."

"Did he say anything when you guys went into his study?"

"He was confused," Seth says. "He kept bringing up something about a clock and keeping the right time. He pointed to a picture of us and said that we were all late.

Then he made me hold his shotgun to see if it was the right size."

"He made me do the same thing."

"I didn't know what to say."

"I'm supposed to take the painting over the mantle," Henry says.

"I fucking hate this."

Both men look to the barge. It moves so painfully slow that it seems as if it will never make it out of sight.

Seth told Elvis all about the wolves over beers on his back porch last week. Elvis told Seth about beavers. Elvis is six and a half feet tall, three-hundred pounds of perfect musculature, and never stops moaning over the beavers.

"Wolves eat beavers," Seth said and scratched Mingus behind the ear.

"That right?" Elvis asked. "Goddamn."

"Yep. Mostly in spring and fall." Seth gulped his beer. "That's when the beavers spend more time on the banks. You know, cutting down trees."

"Fuck I know." Elvis crushed his can. "Goddamn vermin. Do we have any wolves in Virginia?"

"Afraid not." Seth handed Elvis another beer. "But there's going be a pack of them at the docks in Norfolk next week."

Elvis cracked his beer and motioned for him to continue while he drank, his beard so thick that spills bead up like dew.

"From Russia," Seth said. "There's a guy in Wisconsin who had the wolves shipped over so he could turn them loose."

"Why the hell would anybody do a thing like that?"

"I told you," Seth said. "He wants to add to the gene pool. Bolster the health of the population. He's a smart guy. Enthusiastic as hell."

"Goddamn." Elvis stood up and stamped his massive

boot. Mingus flicked his ears and barked. "How can I get me some?" He grinned and craned his neck forward. "Wolves eat goddamn beavers."

"You can't get any wolves, Elvis." Seth finished his beer and retrieved another. "You have to have all sorts of credentials and paperwork. Research studies, numbers, corporate and government grants. All that shit takes years. You're no Doc Conrad."

"Hell with Conrad. We need wolves right here." Elvis spat tobacco juice into Seth's dead garden. "Goddamn."

"That would be something," Seth said. "Wolves in Virginia."

The doctor asks if there is anyone Seth should call. He's called Henry, but not Fran. Seth walks to the little gray phone cubicle, sits down, and punches the numbers. Henry said he was already on his way. Fran hasn't spoken to her father in six years.

"Fran?"

"Yes."

"Fran, it's Seth."

"Oh Seth, it's so good to hear from you."

"Dad's in the hospital."

"I'm sure he is."

"This is serious."

"Did he kill anyone?"

"No."

Seth pauses for Fran to say something, but she doesn't. "Come on, Sis."

"How's Devon?"

"I wouldn't know," Seth says.

The distance between siblings crackles on the line.

In the intensive care unit, the father lies on a gurney enclosed by blue and white curtains. Seth stands next to the gurney with his legs pressed up against the metal guardrails. The father looks right at him and asks in a shaky voice just who in the hell Seth is. He reaches for a chest pocket, but the hospital gown doesn't have one. His cigarettes, of course, are not there either. Two other patients lie in the room. They have curtains as well, but the noise of machines beeping and pumping, of heavy, uncomfortable breathing, and the occasional fragments of mumbling pass right through. The nurse tells Seth that they want to get his father stable and into his own room quickly. She says they'll need privacy.

"The tumor in his liver has swollen to the size, well, to the size of a grapefruit," she says. "The cancer has metastasized."

"What does that mean?"

"Just that it's spread to other parts of his body. Liver, lungs, throat. It's in his blood. We're checking on his lymph nodes as well."

"Christ," Seth says. "He didn't give us specifics. We knew he was sick. Really sick. He made that clear. But he also made it sound like this would go on for a while." Seth shoves his hands in his pockets. "How much time does he have?"

"The doctor will talk to you about that. They have to run more tests. It is possible that treatments will be ineffective at this stage."

"Christ," he says and moves to the door. "I'll be right back."

In the hospital bathroom, small printed signs above the urinals say "Please Conserve Water," but Seth flushes anyway. As he zips up, one of the stall doors opens. Slowly, the top half of a balding head emerges. When the man's eyes appear, they lock on Seth. His head pulls back fast and the door slams shut. Seth listens to the lock click into place.

At the sink, another sign reminds patrons to conserve

water. Seth cups his hands and rinses his mouth. A plastic pump bottle of anti-bacterial gel sits in place of the soap, so he uses it. His hands feel more than clean. They feel sterile. Alabama has been under drought conditions for months. In Virginia, it's even worse.

Seth looks up to see the bald man in the mirror, climbing over the side of the stall. His eyes are darting back and forth between the next stall and Seth's back. It looks like he's wearing pajamas. His arms shake as he teeters on the steel divider. When he realizes Seth sees him, he drops all at once, one leg dunking into the toilet below. He lets out a high-pitched yelp and water splashes from under the stall door.

"You okay?" Seth asks.

"No," he says, finally stepping out of the stall. "I'm all wet."

The bald man's eyes look to Seth with childlike guilt. He is wearing thin hospital clothes. The green pants cling to his skinny legs.

"Don't tell them," he suddenly pleads. "Don't tell them where I am. Don't tell them I'm all wet."

"Okay," Seth says. "I won't tell."

"Thank you. Oh, thank you." The bald man smiles and steps toward Seth as if he might shake hands, but he hears something outside the bathroom and retreats to his stall. He locks the door and lifts his legs out of view.

Elvis claims the first one was easy. His buddy, Hands, who works at the docks and is reputed to have bootlegged more black market whiskey into the country than any man alive, provided the gate pass and key. Inside, he simply opened the crate, lifted the anesthetized wolf, carried him to his pickup, and locked him in a cage he keeps for his dogs. After that, Elvis said, things got tricky.

Dr. Conrad showed up at the Norfolk docks at three in

the morning. He planned on stopping midway for the night, but the anticipation of finally seeing his wolves firsthand pushed him on. He imagined himself comforting the wolves in their uprooted and drugged state. He liked to think that they would remember his kindness in the wild. That they might approach him as a loyal dog approaches his master. In time, the wolves could adopt him as the alpha male, allowing him to control the pack's movement into the most remote areas of Wisconsin. Counting on his knowledge of local pack distribution and following the blips of tagged specimens, he could then shun some of his pack members such that the outcast wolves would integrate into other packs, mate, and begin new genetic lines with superior health. Once Conrad had reduced his pack to the core members, he planned to shed his clothes, drop to all fours, and return to what he now considered his natural state. Conrad drove straight through from Wisconsin, smoking cigars and drinking coffee, and arrived just in time to discover Elvis Moon, a wolf under each arm, turning up a beer by holding it with his teeth.

Dr. Conrad ran to Elvis on adrenaline and kicked him in the crotch. Elvis dropped to his knees and let go of the wolves. The beer bottle clicked off his teeth and shattered on the cement. Conrad only managed to get one wolf back into the crate before Elvis regained composure and hit him in the jaw. The impact of the blow lobbed Conrad's cigar onto the second wolf. Conrad began screaming and lunged for Elvis' throat. Elvis held him back by the shoulders and kicked Conrad in the gut. Conrad crumpled. His breathing sounded like torn bellows. By now, the cigar on the second wolf burned through her dense coat, scorching the skin. The wolf twitched, shook off the cigar, and lifted her head. Elvis leaned over Conrad. The wolf, fighting tranquilizers, stood and took a woozy step toward the two men. She growled. Elvis, who already had one wolf, turned and ran.

The byline in the Tuesday *Norfolk Daily* read, "Stolen Wolf: Ecology Expert Found Sleeping Naked with Remaining Pack."

At his father's house, Seth goes through the mail. Magazines and bills. He stacks the magazines on his desk and opens the bills one at a time. When he gets to the credit card bill, Seth pauses to scan through the charges. His father owes money from stops at the gas station, grocery store, restaurants, and bars. The Black Oyster, Boo Radley's, Wintzell's, and an all night cabaret called Hothouse. The bill at Hothouse is just under five-hundred dollars.

"What the hell costs five-hundred dollars at a cabaret?" Seth asks out loud.

"What?" Henry calls out from the kitchen. He drove to the father's house first. Henry was briefly a ballplayer for the minors. Now he sells cars in Mobile. He says he got lost trying to find the hospital.

"To hell with this." Seth tosses the bills onto the desk.

"What?" he asks again.

"Nothing."

Henry comes in with beers. He looks just like their father. Seth takes a beer and swallows half of it. "You pay the bills. I can't do it."

"Ok," he says. "You call Fran."

"I already tried," Seth says. "I called from the hospital."

"Fuck her," he says.

"Hey," Seth says. "I'm pissed too."

"Yeah, but you're here."

"It's all the same to him."

"He'll come around. I bet he'll know who you are tomorrow." Henry looks up at Seth. "Have you talked to Devon?"

"No, she said not to call."

"Call anyway," Henry says.

Seth starts to respond but finishes the beer instead.

"I had a dream about Devon," Seth says.

In the dream, she lay next to Seth in bed, white T-shirt just down to her hips with her head between the pillows. Seth was propped up against the headboard. Then Devon sat up and draped a rosary over his head. The cross and beads were carved from rough stone. Sandstone maybe. Something porous that felt like sandpaper. The stones were earth colors, from bone white to burnt sienna. Seth felt the weight of the stones on his bare chest. Devon pushed the beads down harder with her hand. They scraped against his skin, but he could also feel the warmth of her fingers and palm. Devon said it was very important for him to have these. Seth isn't religious, but the stones were somehow comforting. He liked the weight.

"In the dream, Devon gave me some kind of rosary," Seth says. "I think it was made out of sandstone."

"Where is she now?" Henry asks.

"She moved to the other side of the mountain." Seth stands up to get another beer. "She rented a little cottage. I miss her."

"Huh," Henry says. "Grab me a beer while you're in there."

Seth brings back the beers and sets one in the middle of the table. Henry has to stand up to get it.

"I don't think they make rosaries out of stone," he says. "Don't they have to be carved from wood?"

"No," Seth says. "I don't know about sandstone, but you can get them in all sorts of other styles. I saw some on the internet. Turquoise, tiger's eye, pearls, quartz. The Vatican sells them right online. You can even request to have yours blessed by the pope. It costs more."

"No shit," he says.

"Did Dad go in for that stuff?" Seth asks. "I don't mean internet rosaries, but church on Sundays, communion, that sort of thing."

"I don't know. He never talked about it." Henry picks at the label on his beer. "I think I saw him cross himself when Clinton was elected."

"I bet he's thinking about it now," Seth says. "I bet everyone thinks about it when you get this close."

Seth wakes up sweating, having dreamt of the wolf. His father's house is so dark that for a moment, he forgets he's in Alabama. He curls into the sheets and reaches for Devon before he remembers and jerks out of bed. Seth makes coffee and heads for the hospital. He parks on the top level of the deck and walks to the elevator. He pushes the button and waits.

"Hey."

"Hello?" Seth says and turns around.

"Hey." A balding head pokes out from behind a Mercedes.

"Have you told?" He steps out from the shadows.

"What?"

"Have you told them about me? You have. They're after me. I've heard them calling my name."

"Who?"

"White coats," he says. "You told. They're after me."

"No," Seth says. "I haven't told anyone."

"Did you know they keep the bodies in the basement?" he asks.

"The morgue," Seth says.

"That's code," he says. "It really means Medulla Oblongata Removal and Grafting Enterprise." He glances over his shoulder and adds, "They're stealing brains."

"Oh," Seth says. "What does the 'u' stand for?"

"I haven't figured it all out. Not yet."

"Oh."

"You told them," he whispers through gritted teeth. "You're one of them."

"No," Seth says. "They have my father. I'm here for my father."

"Liar," he says. "You don't have a father. You just want that man's insides. You're one of them. Thief!" The bald man leans forward, spits at Seth, and runs for the darkness.

The father lies still with tubes stemming from his nose and forearm. Another tube trails out from under the sheets. His stomach is so swollen, even lying on his back, that it seems as artificial as a costume. His hands twitch. Seth sits and watches the muted television screen. Oprah is talking to Regis, but it's impossible to tell who is playing host and who is playing guest.

Henry steps in halfway. "Am I interrupting anything?"

"No," Seth says. "He's not conscious."

"Any news?"

"No. The doctors haven't been by yet." Seth finds the remote and shuts off the television. "What's that?"

Henry sets down a garish arrangement of flowers on the table.

"I don't know what else to do," he says.

Seth shrugs.

"Have you called Devon?" Henry asks.

"Yeah," Seth says. "She has Mingus while I'm gone. Said he's doing fine."

"Anything else?"

"She called me a selfish fuck."

"Oh," he says.

Seth considers turning the television back on. "I wonder if Dad would have cancer if he hadn't smoked and drank so much? I mean, do you think some people are just marked for it."

"I don't understand," Henry says.

"Do you think it's in our blood?" Seth asks. "Our genes?"

"I hope not. But if it is, you and I need to get our hands on some of those internet rosaries. Pay extra and get them blessed by the pope."

The father mumbles something and lifts one hand. He looks as if he might hail Hitler, but then the hand drops and his face goes slack.

Elvis made it back to Free Union by daylight. He called and told Seth to meet up behind his doublewide. Seth asked why, and he said, "You got to see this wolf!" Seth didn't ask any more questions. He was still up after a sleepless night. He had called Devon and asked when he could drop off Mingus again. Seth twisted the cap of a scotch bottle on and off three times before she spoke.

"Anytime before five. Just leave him in the backyard." She paused. "How's your father?"

"Dead."

"I'm sorry, Seth."

"I am too."

"Why didn't you just stay down there?" she asked.

"I don't know."

"I hope you're not drinking."

"Not much," Seth said. "Mingus is getting his winter coat."

"Not much?"

"It's thick. He was so small last winter you couldn't tell." Mingus looked up at Seth from the floor.

"Will you talk to me please?" she asked.

Seth uncrossed his legs and passed the phone from one ear to the other.

"I could cook something for us when I stop by?" he said.

"No," Devon said. "I won't be here."

Then she hung up. Seth stared at the bottle of scotch until the phone, still off the hook, began to beep. He returned it to the cradle and picked up the bottle. He poured one shot into a glass and the rest into the sink. His stomach fell into knots. Mingus rolled over, scratching his back on the rug. Seth sat next to him on the floor, rubbed his belly, and leaned against the kitchen cabinet. The cooling night had chilled the stone floor. Seth moved onto the rug and lay next to Mingus. Holding his paws, Seth closed his eyes and tried to bring Devon's face to mind. Nothing came. So he thought about his sister. Nothing. Then he thought about the scotch, but forced himself to focus on Fran. He stayed there through the night, listening to Mingus breathe, and found that his dog's paws smell like wet leather. Seth wondered if the paws of a wolf smell the same.

When Seth pulled into the drive, Elvis was holding up what looked like a calendar to the cage. He pointed to the picture above the grid, bared his teeth, and chomped at the air. Seth parked and walked over.

"What's with the calendar?" Seth asked.

"They come in the mail," he said. "My little girl loves them. Guess what this month's animal is?"

"Beaver," Seth said.

"Damn straight."

The wolf, no longer medicated, dug at the corners of the cage until his paws bled. No one wanted to open the gate. Seth suggested they carry the cage to the edge of the woods and tie a rope to the latch. So they did, and from fifty feet away, swung open the wire door. The wolf froze. Elvis looked at the wolf, then at Seth, then back at the wolf. He took a step forward.

"Go get them goddamn beavers!" he yelled.

The wolf eased his head out of the cage, took a last look our way, and bolted into the woods.

"I have a plane to catch," Seth said.

"How many beavers do you think he'll eat?" Elvis asked.

"I don't know," Seth said. "Maybe he'll eat them all."

Seth stacks firewood on the back porch. The acorns have fallen and cover the brick patio. Enough leaves have shed that he can see the Indian River, a creek really, slinking down a crease in this ragged mountain. Seth stacks the last of it, maybe a cord and a half—not nearly enough for the coming winter—and sweeps up the bark and beetles from the floor. It's been an hour since his plane landed. It's been a day since the funeral. Seth grabs a bucket and mop, heads upstairs, and lifts some chairs onto the bed. He mops violently for twenty minutes. He returns the chairs. He puts away the mop and grabs a cloth and oil. Seth wipes down everything made of wood. Chairs, chest, bookshelves, coffee table, kitchen table, desk, and lock box. His grandfather made the box for Seth when he was a child. He had pleaded for a pirate's treasure chest, and the grandfather gave him what he asked for. Inside, Seth keeps family pictures. From his great-grandfather standing proudly over a dead bear to a profile shot of Linda's pregnant belly. He wipes down the box once a week. The cabin smells strong of oil now and he puts it away. Thirty more minutes have passed. He heads back downstairs, sprays and wipes the windows. He does the same upstairs. It takes ten minutes. Seth sweeps the acorns from the patio. He uses Comet on the bathtub. Twenty minutes. He digs out last year's ashes from the black iron woodstove. Eight minutes. His hands are blackened with soot. Seth walks out to the garden, dead already, and sprinkles the ashes all over. Devon told him ash is good for the soil. He takes a shovel and works it into the hard ground. He cuts back dead stems of basil and oregano. He churns fruitless tomato plants back into the earth. The garden was Devon's passion, and Seth doesn't know how to maintain it. He lifts the shovel over his head and smashes down dead pepper plants. He smacks them flat. Seth swings at the unplucked cabbage and kicks through the corn stalks. He's about to go after the eggplant when a movement in the woods catches his eye.

Seth steps out of the garden, shovel in hand, and heads toward the river. He walks fifty yards. The water is just a trickle. The wolf stands at the other side, watching him. Seth takes hold of the shovel's handle, swings hard, and slams the metal wedge into the base of a white oak. The impact sends a shock to his elbows and wrists; the ringing blast peals out into the woods like bells. The wolf jumps, cowers, and turns an anxious circle. He's unsure of which way to run. Seth hits it again, harder. The woods fill with sound. Seth hits the oak harder still and his elbows throb, his wrists burn, his ears buzz. Finally the wolf runs, heading north, his silvery back disappearing into turning leaves. Seth hopes instinct will tell the wolf to keep going, keep heading north. Dr. Conrad told him that some wolves, he called them dispersers, travel hundreds of miles from their original home. Maybe Wisconsin isn't too far.

One last time, Seth swings the shovel.

JAKE

As much as I hate to admit it, Dad had a dog. A fine dog. A good dog.

All right, a great dog.

One of those once-in-a-lifetime dogs who will look you in the eye and understand not just what you say, not just the command, but what you mean. A dog who takes in the more complicated human tonalities and converts them into action.

Dad named Jake, like all good southern dogs, for an aspect of hunting life. In this case, a young male turkey. A seasoned hunter will let the Jake pass. It is considered preferable to kill an old gobbler, one with a beard long enough to spot at more than fifty yards, the signal flag for a proper kill. Dad's Jake was an American Labrador. Black. By breeding standards, he was too big. One hundred and ten pounds. By southern hunting standards, Jake was the best thing on four legs in all of Alabama. Dad told stories about Jake. Jake and ducks, Jake and turkeys, Jake and whitetail deer. From the sound of it, Jake could recite hunting laws to the game warden by case number while gumming a mallard and tracking a ten-point buck.

Jake was a dog who would walk with you, not ahead of you. Who would wait for you at the bottom of a flight of stairs, or the top, depending on which direction you were headed. Jake was a dog who could smell the verve in your voice and know in advance if he would be going along in the car or staying behind to guard the house.

Jake did not whine.

If Jake needed to go out in the middle of the night, which was only if Dad forgot his evening walk, he sidled up to bedside and stared, willing you awake to open the door. If that didn't work, he looked for an exposed hand and gave a gentle lick. This would be enough, he knew, to animate Dad into action without anger.

The hard part of this story, the part I don't like to admit, reveals itself here: Dad stepped out into the front yard with a tennis ball in his right hand, and, as I imagine it, with a fresh beer in his left. Jake sat, waiting patiently for Dad to open the beer, take a long swallow, and then toss the ball as high and as far as he could. Jake set out running, lean and fast and entirely focused. He tracked the ball by shadow, anticipating the trajectory of its fall, and prepared for the moment of climax that surely would follow.

It's just bad luck. How could anyone have prevented that ball from landing on a chipped corner of red brick, taking a funny bounce into the sloping yard north of the drive? Who could have told Jake not to follow through, not to jump for the ball off that unpredicted bounce? How could Dad have known that when Jake returned to earth, the fuzzy yellow ball gripped tightly in his mouth, that his rear legs would land first, sliding on layers of oak leaves and pine straw, and that the reality of a heavy dog and a fragile spine would end everything right then and there?

This is how I imagine what happened next: Dad returned from the vet's office empty handed, informed two young boys that Jake would not be coming home, and walked into the kitchen for a drink. There might have been two or three cases of beer on hand, but somehow the bottle of bourbon on the top shelf seemed more appropriate. So down it came, off with the cap, and into the glass. One deep swallow. Then another.

All I know is this: If I threw a tennis ball for my dog Blue, and Blue never came back, I'd take that drink too. I'd pull down the bottle from the top shelf and pour the tallest glass I could find. There's nothing that could ease that kind of hurt, but I think I'd try. But then again, I don't have two boys to tell, and I know my wife would need that drink worse than me.

The truth is, it might not have happened that way. It might have been completely different. I've been in the car with Dad enough times to know that a late night, a bottle of bourbon, and a dark driveway could easily end with a very dead dog. So maybe he lied. Eventually, everyone reaches a state of constant disbelief. Because when an Alabama hunter starts talking, when he gets long-winded and pink in the cheeks and gestures wildly with his hands, you never know how much of it is fact. You never know how much of it is story.

SPANISH AND KING

I want to tell you my fishing story. If you think you've already heard it, you probably have. But don't worry. It's different every time.

Shane Purvis has a birthmark across his face. Instead of too much pigment, he has none at all. It forms the shape of a cartoon ghost creeping up from under his collar and reaching out to his nose. The kids call him Leper and Whitewash behind his back. Sometimes I do too. His son Tripper and I are best friends. Tripper, of course, is really Shane Purvis III, but we won't start calling him Shane until high school. And only then when he demands it. Most kids call him Shrimper. Mrs. Purvis had a problem with her pregnancy, something called preeclampsia, so Tripper is half my size. He was a one-pound preemie who never caught up. Mr. Purvis stands six-feet tall with broad shoulders and doesn't seem to notice his boy is so small. And in two years he won't be. One day after gym class, it will be revealed that Tripper is bigger than anyone. His nickname will instantly switch to Moby. Girls, even the older ones, will giggle and blush as they walk by. Some will let their eyes drop.

Right now, Mr. Purvis and Tripper and I take turns baiting hooks with live porgies and tossing out the line. We troll

across rolling gulf swells, watching the places where the
lines and water meet.

"Spanish mackerel been running pretty good," Mr. Purvis
says.

"What about King?" I ask.

"Sure, some King too. But mainly Spanish."

"I want a Marlin," Tripper says.

"Like you could reel that in," I say.

Tripper flips me off.

"No Marlin this close to shore, Tripper," Mr. Purvis says.
"We'd have to get out past the oil rigs and use some bigger
tackle."

"Have you got bigger tackle?" I ask.

"At the house," Mr. Purvis says. "Not on the boat. Not
today."

"But we can catch King, right?" I ask.

"Sure can."

"What about Tuna?" Tripper asks.

"Maybe, but I ain't seen much of them lately." Mr. Purvis
rubs sun-block on his birthmark and stares at the horizon.
"Bonito maybe. I've seen them."

Tripper and I open Cokes and bags of pretzels. We throw
a few overboard and watch to see if they float or sink. They
float. I ask Mr. Purvis if I can drive the boat again.

"Sure, Ben. It's fine out here. I didn't want you to drive
in the harbor what with all them other boats, but out here is
just fine. Pick out a point on the horizon, check your
compass, then keep her straight. And not too fast for trolling.
Good. No problem at all."

Mr. Purvis wraps his big hands over my shoulders and
kneads them. It hurts, but I don't say it. I check the compass,
due west, and keep an eye on the digital Fishfinder. Little
black dots appear on the screen, but nothing hits the lines.
I keep us heading west.

In the bow, Mr. Purvis arm wrestles Tripper. They lock

arms over the ice chest and their butts wag in the air. I can tell Mr. Purvis isn't trying, but Tripper's face has gone entirely red. He does a sort of tap dance and shakes his head, then howls for more strength. Mr. Purvis drops to both knees, feigns agony, and lets his arm fall. Tripper hoots and jumps up and down. He pumps his fist and says, "You lose, sucker!" I steer the boat.

Then the drag on the port side reel begins to click. A slow ticking at first, then a sizzle of line explodes from the spool. Mr. Purvis runs past me to the stern and grabs the rod. He lifts it from the gunnel-hole and sets the hook. He gives the crank a few turns, then hands it over to Tripper.

"Slow her down a bit," Mr. Purvis says over his shoulder. He reels in the other lines and puts them away.

I turn around and pull back the throttle a quarter-inch. Tripper holds the butt of the rod between his legs to keep the tip from dipping down. From where I'm standing, it looks like he's taking a shit. I check the compass and see that I've let us drift. I steer back to due west and keep it there. Tripper squeezes his eyes closed and does his best to reel in line. His face goes red. Then, as if told to do so, the fish tires and Tripper pulls him in.

"A good size Spanish, I'd bet," Mr. Purvis says. "Throw it in neutral."

I pull the throttle back into neutral, but it stays in gear. I'm not sure how it works, so I turn the key and kill it. Mr. Purvis takes the gaff and eases it along the side of the boat, sinking the hook beneath rushing water. Tripper reels the last few feet and pulls the Spanish alongside the boat. Mr. Purvis gaffs him and lifts the Spanish out of the water and into the sun. His iridescent back glimmers with specks of gold, but I watch the blood run from mouth and gills to a dull white belly.

"Oh, baby!" Tripper shouts.

"Five. Five and a half pounds," Mr. Purvis says. "See

this speck a black on the dorsal fin? That's how we know it's a Spanish and not a little baby King. Little King's are called snakes. Snow birds on rented boats catch snakes and think they got a Spanish worth keeping. Don't even know it's a baby King until they get written up."

Mr. Purvis uses pliers to remove the hook and tosses the Spanish into the ice chest with one hand. He pats Tripper on the back, and forgetting himself, kisses the top of his head. Tripper ducks down and pretends it didn't happen.

"I pity the fool gets on *my* line!" Tripper says.

"You're up," Mr. Purvis says. He looks at me and smiles. I nod. Then he notices the engine is off.

"Don't kill the engine out here, Ben. Just put her in neutral. If she don't start up again, we'll be in a heap a trouble."

I mouth the words *Aye-aye, Captain Whitewash,* but I'm facing the other way.

The engine starts on the first try and we backtrack to find the school of Spanish. I bait hooks and let out the line from the other rods while Tripper sloshes his hands in the bait-well, trying to catch porgy without a net.

"I'm after King," I say. "A big ole King, a hundred pounds."

"You know what they call the big ones?" Mr. Purvis asks.

"No," I say.

"Smokers," he says. "They hit so hard that smoke'll come right off your line. And it'll feel like a hundred pounds, sure enough."

Tripper gives up and scoops a porgy into the net. He holds the oily fish an inch from his mouth and whispers, "You lose, sucker. Now go get the King."

He throws out the line.

This time last year, Dad said he'd take me fishing. I made tuna sandwiches and he filled the ice chest with beer. We each held an end of the cooler and took our time getting it to the end of the dock.

I know. Another fishing story. And I haven't even finished the last one. But you haven't heard this before. I never tell this story.

"I don't cry over spilled milk," Dad said, "but I sure as hell cry over spilled beer."

I didn't think it was funny, then or now, but I laughed anyway. It's a laugh I learned from Dad; a polite, *Okay, good one*, without actually having to talk.

We went back to the house and gathered up rods and reels, thousands of dollars in tackle. Dad finished a beer and popped another while we chose rods. He wore loose canvas shorts and exposed himself every time he sat or kneeled. He may or may not have known it. I looked away. Instead, I focused on picking the biggest rod I saw, not knowing if it was right for our trip. I didn't know where we were going. I didn't know what we were fishing for. Dad laughed.

"Try this one, Mr. Big-man," he said. "You'll have an easier time with it."

He handed me an old Zebco. Olive green with rusty guides. I took it without looking up.

"Can you catch King Mackerel with this?"

"You bet," he said.

I said nothing.

"I'll try this one today," he said, picking up a brand new spinning rod. The translucent red stem cut the air as Dad made a faux cast. "I found this little jewel in Point Pilot. They robbed me blind, but Goddamn, just look at it."

We took our gear and walked back down to the dock. I'd already lowered the boat from the lift, unhooked the steel cables, and tied up to the gang-walk cleats. I darted back and forth stowing this here and that there; everything in its place. I wedged life jackets between tackle boxes so they wouldn't bang or spill as we motored out. I used twist ties to make sure the rods would stay in place. I worked fast but made sure not to drop anything. When I was done, Dad thumped his cigarette into the bay.

"That seat cushion will blow off," he said. "Sit on it or stow it."

"I was about to sit on it."

"Then let's hit it," he said. "We'll head for the rock jetty and pull up Reds."

Then he looked down and put a hand on his stomach. The wind churned up a light chop and the boat knocked against rubber bumpers. Inside the boat, nothing moved.

"Hang on," he said.

I watched the sky as a flock of brown pelicans drifted in from the south. They flew in single file and landed one by one at the base of a floating buoy. They bent their yellowed heads at strange angles to preen. The last pelican, a slow-moving straggler, dove entirely underwater and surfaced with a fish.

"Hang on," Dad said again, still holding his stomach.

He trotted back down the dock towards the house. I didn't understand, so I followed him. Just as he reached the point on the dock where it transitions from water to land, Dad froze. Both hands lurched for his stomach. Then, just as suddenly, shit ran down his legs.

I froze too, of course. I didn't say a word. Dad looked over his shoulder in rage, then back at his legs. He hobbled down the steps to the beach, kicked out of his shoes, and made short little steps to the water.

I ran into the house. We did not speak of it. We did not go fishing.

I didn't know it then, but I have since learned that when a son witnesses a father beshit himself, it is a psychological rite of passage. The textbook actually used the word *beshit*. The idea is that the father has reached a point in life where he can no longer take care of himself, much less his family, and the son must assume that role. From what I read, this is a natural occurrence. *Progressive difficulties with continence and toileting occur...the subject beshits himself...middle adults may experience mild trauma...can achieve proper maturation through conscious and subconscious acceptance.* Told this way, the rite of passage makes sense. But I couldn't find anything about a young boy watching his drunk father *beshit* himself, so I try not to think about it.

At this point in the story, you'd probably like to know if I caught that big King or not. Truth be told, I did. Forty pounds hit the line fast and hard and we even think we saw a little smoke coming up from the reel. I fought him for thirty-seven minutes. When I reeled him in to boatside, you might expect one of two things. Either I hold the rod upright with one arm and gaff the King with the other—raising the fish into the boat with a tumult of cheers and clapping behind me—or I look down into the water, feeling pangs of guilt and sympathy, and decide on the spot that I must release him. Also to cheers and clapping. Either way, the story ends here: the emblematic fish either served up for supper or swimming to freedom, depending on which metaphor suits my mood. Often, I consider my audience.

But today I've decided on another ending.

It goes something like this:

Mr. Purvis takes the wheel and I stay back with the rods. Tripper eats more pretzels and occasionally opens the cooler to look at his fish. He holds the lid open with one arm and pumps his fist with the other.

I stand up at the stern of the boat, looking down on the churning water. The motor hums evenly until it chews through an occasional clump of seaweed. The water just behind the boat turns a darker shade of green as diced stems and leaves rise to the surface. The sun, now directly overhead, casts no shadows. It is hot. My shoulders are burned and I know by the time we get home, they will blister. I sit down. We wait.

For an hour we troll. Tripper creates a tent with a beach towel and bait net, and sits Indian style, flipping through comic books. Mr. Purvis puts up the shade over the steering wheel and watches the Fishfinder. He opens another coke and presses the can to his face. I put one hand on the closest rod and shut my eyes. For a few seconds, I think I'm asleep.

"So how's your Dad's new house?" Mr. Purvis asks.

"It's all right," I say.

"He has a boat lift, right? I'd kill for my own lift."

"Yeah."

"You been fishing yet?"

I open my eyes and stare at the motionless spool of line.

"Yeah," I say. "Last year. We got Spanish and King."

"No way," Tripper says.

"Yes way," I say. "In the bay."

"Spanish and King don't run in the bay," Mr. Purvis says. "Not enough salt."

"I meant the Gulf. We got fourteen Spanish and one King."

"No way," Tripper says.

"How is your Dad?" Mr. Purvis asks. "I heard they have a new baby."

"Did you catch the King?" Tripper asks.

"Yeah," I say. "He fought like crazy."

"No way."

"How much do you see them?" Mr. Purvis asks.

"I go over there all the time. Dad says he's going to buy me a boat."

"No way," Tripper says.

I start to respond, but the motor lurches and begins to whine. Mr. Purvis shoves the throttle into neutral and pushes a button to raise the prop. He rushes back to where I'm sitting and looks down into the water. As the prop rises, a tangle of trawling net appears, and hanging from the edge, a severed human hand.

I've heard stories of fishermen losing fingers and hands. They find themselves in the wrong place at the wrong time and a line pulls taut, fast as a bullet, and just like that it's gone. Or more likely, there's the winch. It's always the winch that sucks you in. Or maybe a surimi auger catches on your cuff and pulls you wrist-deep into grinding metal. People say the bait chopper on a crabbing boat will take off your fingers and leave the stump. But I've never met a one-handed man. I've never sat in a bar in Mobile or Dauphin Island or Gulf Shores and seen anyone with a hook or claw. I look for them. Ever since that hand showed up in our engine, I have been compelled to seek out the man who lost it.

But in the moment it happens, I scream. The hand is swollen, ghost-white, and pockmarked from feeding fish. I jump back and hide in the front of the boat. I avert my eyes and hyperventilate.

Tripper cries out, "No way!"

"Holy shit," Mr. Purvis says.

"This is the coolest fishing trip ever," Tripper says.

"Holy shit," Mr. Purvis says.

"Cut it loose," I say.

"No. No, wait. I think. I think. We better take it back with us."

"Oh, baby!" Tripper says.

I watch the horizon while Mr. Purvis scoops up the hand. He goes to great lengths not to touch it. He bags it and throws it on ice. Tripper dances around the cooler and beats his chest with tiny clenched fists. They take turns opening the lid and staring.

"Do you think a shark bit it off?" Tripper asks.

"If he did, it'd still be in his belly." Mr. Purvis says. "It's a clean cut. Right through the skin and bone and everything. I'd say that fella was using the header. Those big spinning blades that cut off fish heads like a length of two by four. I heard about a guy who lost his hand that way. A wave hit the boat all the sudden and *bzzzzzt* no more hand. He sued for two million. Story goes."

"Or the mob cut it off." Tripper assumes a weightlifting pose.

"You all right, Ben?"

"Fine," I say. "A little seasick."

"It happens to the best of us." Mr. Purvis winks. "Let's head home."

I can't quite put it all together in my mind, but I'm somehow sure this is my fault. Not the hand, and not going home early. I get that. But this panicky knot in my stomach. This dizziness. This burn in my eyes. I feel shame. And I want off this boat.

What I said before, that part about catching a forty pound King. I lied. This is the true ending. The hand and the sickness and shame. I prefer telling the one with cheers and clapping. I like the way a certain face will light up when I say I ate the King that night, and the way another will soften when I say I threw him back. But it's all fishermen's tales. Stories I've told and been told a thousand times.

Sometimes I just can't bring myself to admit it.

60 Seconds

When my head surfaces and I open my eyes, the propeller churns fourteen inches from my nose. It might be more, maybe a little less, but at this moment, treading water in Soldier's Creek, I settle on fourteen inches. I think, *Shit, propeller, back up, swim,* but instinct takes over and my hands grab the top of the engine. I hold myself away from the blades. The engine cover is hot from the sun, but I grab it tight. I think, *Shit, propeller, my legs,* and feel for the sand with the tips of my toes. The water is too deep to stand. The engine runs in reverse, sucking water toward it, pulling at my legs as they dangle, unable to secure firm footing. The engine chugging fills my ears and I think, *Call out for help,* but my throat goes dry, my tongue a wad of putty. My wet hands slip down an inch. I freeze like this: arms up, legs out. My knees bend and ankles flex as if I'm driving a straight-shift car. I don't have a straight-shift car, but Graham does. I've watched him drive it. I manage to say, "Graham," but I'm speaking into so much noise. I call out, "Graham!" I can't see over the back of the boat, but I know that Graham is leaning forward in the bow with his big hands clinking the anchor chain into the anchor well. I know the sound of clinking metal and a three-hundred-horsepower engine is drowning out my voice. I try to stand again, but my toes skim the loose sand. The sand feels good between my toes, but I think, *What if Graham never hears me screaming, what if I lose my legs? The prop will cut my legs, then I'll be castrated, then I'll pass out from pain and the prop will grind my body into chum. I wonder if sharks will come.* So I scream, "Graham!" I try to touch the bottom again, but now I can't feel my toes. *Oh shit,* I think, *my legs are rising into the prop.* I stare down into the water, but I can't see much for the swirls of white bubbles and reflected sunlight. I wonder how long I can hold this position. I wonder if anyone on the beach can see me. Shane, Andrew, Eloise and Donna have an ice chest full of beer and a portable radio. They're a hundred yards away. They're just out lying in the hot sun. I think I can hear their music. I think it might be George Jones. I think it might be "The Race is On." I listen carefully, humming it out. *Now the race is on and here comes pride up the backstretch, heartache's a going to the inside...* Yeah, that's what it is. I hate George Jones. I'm thinking, *Goddamn that little radio is loud.* I'm thinking, *Turn that shit off and save my ass! Can't you jack-off's see I'm about to fucking die!* Then I realize I'm not thinking this, but yelling it. I'm screaming with all the air I've got. And that's when the first one hits me. It feels like a thump. I'm sixteen years old. I jerk my legs backward but this position is so awkward and I can't control my body like I think I should. I think, *Maybe I imagined it.* My head spins dizzy and my shoulders burn. Sweat fills my eyes. But my left leg aches, so I'm thinking *This must be real.* It's my left leg, so I know the thump came from the flat side of the propeller blade turning down. My right leg will get the sharp edge turning up. I think, *That's going to hurt a hell of a lot more.* So I scream, "Graham!" I'm thinking, *Why is it in reverse? Why isn't it in neutral? I put it in neutral. I swear to fucking god I put it in neutral. I'm not incompetent. I know how to drive a boat. I grew up on boats. My mother's father built boats for a living, for Christ's sake. Sailboats. Motherfucking sailboats. But you can't hydro-slide behind a sailboat. And that's why we're here. In Shane's boat. His boat is different. The throttle has a trick to it. What was it? Click it up, then out. Did I click it out?* I close my eyes and my head lolls back. I squeeze my eyes tight. I wonder if I should spread my legs further apart. That might prevent another hit to my legs, but the chances of castration seem to increase dramatically. I keep my legs as they are. I'm thinking, *Donna's not even that pretty. She's got buck teeth with a gap. That girl could eat corn on the cob through a chain link fence. And I hate the way she laughs. Sometimes I want to slap her.* I'm also thinking, *Graham must be retarded. And deaf. Meathead. I hope the steroids shrink his dick. It can't possibly take this long to put up the anchor. What the hell is he doing? Can't he see I'm not in the boat? Shit, I'm not supposed to be the in the boat. I'm supposed to be paddling out to the Hydro-slide and waiting at the end of the ski rope. I'm supposed to be ready to go. But he can look out and see I'm not there. He can look out and see the end of the rope and the abandoned Hydro-slide. Why the hell doesn't he know what's going on?* My arms shake. My hips go numb. And that's when the second one hits me. Right leg. Blade turning up. I think, *Funny, it doesn't hurt as much as the first one.* Then I think, *Of course it doesn't hurt as much, it's a clean slice, no bruising, just a long deep cut through the inside of my right leg.* I wonder, *Isn't there an important vein in there?* I wonder if I'll bleed out. I wonder if I'm already dying. The burn in my shoulders is so intense now, I can't feel any pain in my legs. So I scream, "GRAHAM!" I'm thinking, *You're not a meathead. I know you didn't really do steroids; you're just bigger than I am. You've got big hands. It's genetic. Dad is big. I'm built like Mom. Please save me.* I'm thinking, *Look up, Donna. Look up. Look out here and see me. Your teeth are fine. You'll get braces. After that, you won't whistle every time you say* see *or* seems *or* cedar. *Please look up.* I'm wishing I could hold Donna in my aching arms. I'm wishing that she was the one between my legs and not this engine. I'm wishing I could lie down on this quiet beach with our ice chest of stolen beer and listen to George Jones. I think

I hear it again. Yeah, they must have rewound the song. *Now the race is on and here comes pride up the backstretch, heartache's a going to the inside... It* is *a good song,* I think. *It has a nice beat, funny lyrics. I'd like to be on the beach listening to this song. To this very song. I'd drink a stolen beer and thank Graham for stealing it.* But my right leg gets hit again. The sharp edge turning up. And then, at that instant, something changes. The noise is different. I hear a warbling shudder inside the engine. A pop of metal on metal, then silence. The propeller slows and stops on my left leg. One last thump of flat steel against my thigh. My hands slide off the engine and I slip down underwater. I think, *I'll just float here. This feels good. My shoulders feel much, much better.* The water is clear. I open my eyes and I stare at the propeller. I wonder why there's no blood. *There should be bright red clouds of blood. In* Jaws, *it was blood, blood, blood. Du-nuh. Du-nuh, nuh-nuh. But this is so much water and I have skinny little legs. Bird legs. Maybe I need steroids. My hands are small. I need air.* I'm thinking, *I'll drown if I stay like this.* So I stroke my arms and push my head through the surface. I fill my lungs with air. Graham leans over the stern of the boat with an outstretched hand. His eyes are open wide and all the color has drained from his face. I can hear George Jones clearly now, and it's "The Race is On." I'd like to sit on the beach and listen to it with buck-toothed Donna. I'd like to open a stolen beer and pretend it tastes good. I'd like to lie in the sun. I'm thinking how good it would feel to walk over there with the sand between my toes and lie down in the hot, hot sun.

So I take my brother's hand.

NEIGHBORS

T he apartment door clicking shut wakes me. Audrey walks in, smoking. She drops her cigarette into a beer bottle on the nightstand and lifts her gray sweater up and over her head. Feeling safe in the darkness, she unhooks her bra, exposing small breasts, eggshell white within triangles of a winter-faded tan. I watch her surreptitiously, my eyes fully adjusted to the night. Audrey pulls one of my t-shirts from the dresser, struggling to find the appropriate holes. She kicks off leather boots and stomps out of her jeans. The trademark logo of Havana 59, the restaurant where Audrey works, is stitched into her panties. She crawls into bed as if her bones are made of rubber. I smell tequila, smoke, perfume, and sex when she presses against me, spooning beneath linen sheets.

"Have fun?"

"I guess. We drank too much."

"I can tell."

"What'd you do?"

"Worked 'til eight. Had a beer at The Garage. Ran into Shane."

"How is he?"

"Bearded."

"Wintertime."

"Yeah."

Audrey clutches at my waist and I can tell she is spinning. She buries her face between my shoulder blades. The smell of her makes me sick, but I don't say it. I reach back and check to be sure she is covered. The alarm clock reads four fifty-two.

"Shit. My pill."

Audrey gets up, becomes dizzy, and claws at the bed for balance. After a second of closed-eyed concentration, she goes to her knees and digs through her purse in the dark. I hear jingles, clicks, and finally, "Got it." She swallows the pill without water and slinks back into bed.

"I wish you had told me you would be so late."

"Why?"

"I worry about you."

"Worry, worry."

"Seriously."

"You're not my boyfriend."

"I know, but…"

"But what?"

I stay silent.

"What's all this?"

Audrey turns so that we lie back to back. Her toes press into my calf and I can't believe how cold they are.

"Nothing."

I sleep fitfully, waking often with my throat becoming sore. I click off the alarm before it erupts, slip out of bed, and tip toe to the shower. I work Saturdays and let Audrey sleep. I dress in the darkness, feeling for my boots and easing out into the den. I leave a note on the coffee table, *Dinner tonight? Stop by at seven. Ben.* But I know that when I get off work, she will be gone. Out with other friends, other men, drinking and standing close. Audrey lives next door, and the proximity is wearing me thin.

I stop by Audrey's to see what she has planned for the weekend. Her roommate Amy answers the door.

"Where's Audrey?"

"Gone, gone, gone, Ben." Amy twirls and sips root beer from the can. Her skin is the color of almonds.

"Where?"

"Skiing. She drove over to Wintergreen and met up with some guy named Charles. She says he's a dentist. I bet he makes good money. I'd like to meet a dentist."

"Yes. Well."

"Want to go down to Havana 59 and get a drink? Audrey says that margaritas are half price right now. We should go get a drink. Don't you need a drink? Come on Ben, you know you want to." Amy twirls again and snatches up her fleece jacket. Behind her, leafless tree branches tick against the window. Frost collects in the corners of the glass panes. Amy purses her lips and blots a napkin against them. She smiles, vermilion red, and latches on to the crook of my arm.

The bar at Havana 59 is crowded with the rich and well groomed. They glow with artificial tans and beaming white teeth. Champagne sits on every other table. A man at a corner table drops to one knee and pulls something from his blazer pocket. I can't see the ring from here, but the woman's shoulders shake and her head bobs. The adjacent tables explode into cheers. I check myself in the mirror behind the bar and wish I hadn't. Amy, however, smiles and twirls and squeezes my hand.

"Margaritas! I want mine frozen, lime, and make sure they put it in one of those funny glasses that look like a goldfish bowl. And a straw. Don't look at me that way." Amy twirls away.

I order without getting into specific types of glasses. A dark, plaintive-eyed girl taps my shoulder, offering up a tray of cigars, but I pass. The girl, wearing a short skirt and halter-top, moves down the bar with manufactured enthusiasm, and I suddenly regret my decision. It is as though I have hurt her in some unseen way. Neon blinks on the girl's face through hazy cigar and cigarette smoke. A white haired fat man buys a cigar and slips the girl a twenty. She tucks the bill into the waist of her skirt. Without pause, she has turned to the next customer, pointed out each variety, and made another sale. "Dominican, Jamaican, Honduran," she says. "And these are from the Canary Islands." The smile rises and falls with each customer, but her eyes—round and dark as coffee beans—never change.

Amy catches up with old friends at the next table. She tugs at her blonde hair and taps a suede cowboy boot. The couple at the table looks up to Amy's face with eyes wide. They grin and laugh and lean forward as she talks. The bartender brings my drink, scotch, and Amy's fluorescent green fishbowl. I am at once embarrassed by the bowl and relieved that the right one came. Amy returns and we drink and talk, our conversation passing from pleasant to intimate as the alcohol works our blood. In a show of bravado, or possibly fear of exclusion, we purchase Honduran cigars. Twelve dollars apiece. The cigar girl winks at me as we step outside. I look back, but the door closes and the girl is gone. Amy lights a match under her cigar and then holds it out for me. I lean in close. The cobbled terrace shimmers in lamplight, the late-night air is cold, and Amy's hand slips into mine.

Back at my apartment, we tear at one another. Clothes coming off, hitting the floor. I pull back the sheets and we're in, grappling and gripping and gasping for air. Our sex is electricity and heat. Ice ticks and pops at the windowpanes. I can't help myself and I imagine she is Audrey, pressing against me. I slide my fingers over her breasts. Cup my hands to the small of her back. I flex my hips. I kiss her mouth, her perfumed neck. I reach for her hands and squeeze. Audrey and I have never done any of this. We drink together, eat together, and for a month now, sleep together, but nothing more. At once I realize I have fallen in love with her. And I'm fucking her roommate like dogs in heat. I open my eyes and look at Amy, flushed and breathless. She lies on her back. Even in moonlight, her breasts are tan as almonds. She pulls me down, as if to whisper in my ear. I bury my face in the pillow.

Audrey returns on Tuesday and I know Amy tells her. I just know. Audrey and Amy live in 3F and I live in 3G. Our doors face one another, squared off like gunfighters. The floor plans are a mirror image. I turned my second bedroom into an office. A roommate would save money, but I loathe living with other guys. I'd live with Audrey if I could. For nearly a week I come and go at times I think I can avoid them both, staying at work as much as I can. I work for Richmond's outdoor outfitter, Blue Mountain. Tents, backpacks, and boots. Compactable stoves that run on white gas and convert into lanterns. We will protect you from the rain, wick away your sweat, and insulate you from the cold.

At the store, Shane lances price tags through double-stitched, chemically treated shirts. I fold. Shane checks his watch.

"You're still here."

"So."

"Are you fucking Audrey yet?"

"What? No. Not exactly."

"You don't want to go home, do you?"

"I'm broke, I need the hours."

"Bullshit."

Shane catches his thumb on the tagging gun and an orb of crimson blood swells between flesh and nail. He presses a paper towel down on it hard.

"What makes you think I want to fuck Audrey?"

"Who wouldn't want to fuck Audrey? Audrey's good

stuff. And didn't you say she was sleeping with you? But 'not sleeping with you,' whatever that means. What are you up to out there?"

"Sure, she sleeps at my place sometimes. Doesn't like sleeping alone. But nothing else. We haven't even kissed."

"What the hell is that?"

"Look, it's good. Not everything is about sex."

"Sure. And now you don't want to go home."

"Whatever."

"You fucked Amy." Shane grabs a handful of red beard and grins.

"No."

"Yes. You fucked Amy."

"Maybe."

"Damn, what was that like? I bet that girl twirls in bed. Good stuff, that twirling. But neighbors. Shit."

"Might be a problem."

"Never fuck a neighbor. That's the rule. You can't escape."

"Hey thanks. Go tape your thumb."

It's late, but Audrey and Amy's door sits open. They leave it that way when they want me to stop over for a drink. I have about six more steps to decide what I should do. Audrey pokes her head out with three steps left.

"I thought I heard you."

"Yeah."

"Where have you been all week? I've got the dirt on you." Audrey points a finger at my chest and cocks her eyebrow.

"Work. Oh."

"Come in, Amy's out."

I step into the apartment and take a seat in the wicker chair near the door. The room is warm. Audrey brings me a beer. She wears her hair down and casual. Her jeans look

new—the way she fits in them, more sensual, more perfect—
and her white silk shirt floats over her breasts, giving me
the illusion of visibility. I look down at my beer.

"So…"

"What, it was stupid. I'm sorry."

"Sorry?"

"Well, she's fun." I pause but don't look up. "How was
your dentist?"

"Charles?"

"Sure, Charles."

"He's my cousin."

"Cousin."

"He's great. We drove over to Wintergreen and went
skiing Saturday. Had a blast. I called in sick Monday so we
could catch a few more runs. You should have seen me on
the blacks. I skied so much better this time." Audrey
scratches the back of her hand with pink fingernails. "I think
I finally learned how to stay in control. I focused on each
turn, paid attention to my weight."

"I'm never sure whether to lean forward or lean back."

"Is something wrong?"

"No."

"Yeah."

"I've just been working too much this week. Inventory."

"Are you going to ask Amy out for this weekend?"

"I don't know."

"Shit."

"What?"

"Don't do this."

I drink my beer and stare at the television while Audrey
lights a cigarette. Clint Eastwood is cutting a guy down with
his Colt. He tells the guy how stupid he is after the guy is dead.

"What are you doing this weekend? Out of town again?"

"No. I thought I'd stick around here. Watch an apartment
fling unfold."

"We could get dinner."

"With Amy?"

"With you."

"I think you better do that with Amy."

"Well."

"Well?"

"Yeah."

Audrey steps to the window and presses her hand against the glass. Ravens in the tree beyond the window eye her movement. After a few seconds of ruffled feathers and muted caws, they fall silent. She pulls her hand away and shakes out the cold.

"I'm wiped out. I think I'll go to bed. You coming?"

"I think you better do that with Amy, too."

"Yeah. Well."

"Yeah."

"Goodnight, Audrey."

I stand up and take a step toward Audrey, but she is already making for the kitchen with the empty beers. I let her go, and walk back into the hall. I stop for a moment between apartments. With both doors shut, I can almost touch them at the same time. I'm an inch shy. The light in the ceiling buzzes, and I look up at the collected moths, trapped and dying in the glass dome. I smell snow as a draft sweeps through the stairwell door. For now, I am content to stand here, in between apartments, neither tenant nor neighbor. It is late, the light flickers, and under the weight of collecting snow, I can hear the rafters groan.

MOVIE NIGHT

Midnight, and it's the Thursday murder movie that's got you started, all nerves and nervous laughter, and of course, there's the pistol on your nightstand. Your father died and there it is; *what to do with it?* Not quite ready to sell his things, not quite sure how to live with them. Your wife thinks a gun is a good idea for country living. And then the dog barks his head off at something down the dark driveway, an unseen animal crashing through the woods, and you're back inside like a shot, dead-bolting the doors and flicking window locks all over the house. But it's late and time for bed and the dog is calm and your wife is already asleep, so you get under covers and try to think about what you might do if you won the lottery, or if you had married a woman who didn't walk all over you, or what your dog might say if he could, and just when your head is filled with talking dogs and endless riches and sleep is creeping in, it's headlights in the driveway that jerk you to the window. A car pulls in and stops with the engine still rattling and coughing, headlights filling the room and before you know it the holstered pistol is in your hand. You make for the front door and turn on the lights and stare through the glass and the dog is barking bloody murder by the time the driver of the car realizes he's at the wrong house and begins to roll backward, crunching gravel and shrinking from view. So you laugh it off and hop in bed next to your motionless wife, pistol back on the nightstand, and you're almost calmed down enough to sleep when you remember the trash truck comes tomorrow and you don't want another fight, so you're back up and dragging ass along the driveway, flashlight in hand, big blue trash can rolling behind you. When the gravel hits pavement, you look up and down this Tennessee road, long and dark and deserted this far out, and count six blue trash cans already waiting. You know there are more, but the farthest ones slip into the blue shadows and blue driveways of this very blue night. At this distance, they could be anything. And then you hear glass break and see lights flipping on and off in the trailer across the street and then it's yelling and the man is backing out the door with his hands up and the woman in her underwear is throwing spatulas and forks. The man gets in his diesel truck and guns it out the drive, but still takes the time to wave at you as he peels past. The woman is standing in the doorway, a thick silhouette bobbing with tears, but you don't know her name so you turn back down the drive and listen when she says, *Fuck you too,* as her door slams shut. The unseen animal crashes through the woods again and your heart stops, sending you running for the house and fumbling with the locks, and then you hear your name called, your wife screaming for you from the bedroom, and when you open the door it hits you like a swarm of stinging bees in the chest and you look down at the blood and up at your wife and she's got the pistol and this look on her face that says, *I knew it was you all along,* and then she starts shaking and the pistol drops from her hand and while the whining dog crawls under the bed you think, *I'm not dead yet,* so you walk over and pick up the gun. For the first time you see it out of the holster and it's a tiny .22 caliber loaded with bird shot, which is the exactly the same as facing a firing squad of little boys packing Daisy Red Riders and then you understand that you're really not dead, not even close, and you look at your hateful wife, and that's when you start laughing hard, raising up the gun to her bare feet and pulling the trigger, because all you can think of is how much better that movie would have been if they'd only thought of this.

NIGHT SWIMMING

to remember Alex Stirling

Session 1

"This is my dream," I say.

"Go ahead."

"Outside of the car on a warm Georgian night, we stripped and dove headfirst into the not-at-all cold water. Fiona giggled and announced that *it must be the water, the water must be cold, it must be the cold water.* Andrew and Delia waited in the backseat of the car, a quiet night, our noises the only break in silence. I splashed water on the hood and screamed for them to *hurry up, it's fine. The water is just fine.* Fiona dove under, allowing her backside to rise up and crest the surface before disappearing again, so moved by recklessness and water. Andrew opened his door and put a foot out. Delia crooned, *Noooooo,* and then laughing, *Yeeeeeeahhhh.* Her door opened. The moon hung low above the lake. A photograph of Andrew's dead father, the priest, sat on the dashboard. Fiona climbed out of the water and grabbed the tire swing. We could see her wet breasts, wet legs, wet everything, and she didn't care. I didn't either. Maybe it was the beer, or maybe the pot, but it seemed to all of us that nothing could induce such freedom, nothing but swimming at night. She screamed, *Come on come on come on,* and Andrew stood up with the car door in front of him. Fiona swung out and let go, a terrific moment without gravity, her body moonlit and motionless, her legs perfectly straight below, her arms straight above, her eyes closed and then, just as planned, she slipped soundless, without splash, into the water. Delia, stood up, car door covering everything, and cried out, *Is it too cold?"*

The psychiatrist stared at me. He wore a suit and bow tie and Italian wingtips. Round spectacles perched at the end of his nose.

"Andrew answered back," I continued. "An unexpected *no! no! no! no! no!,* and took the three long steps across the sandy grass and leapt naked, an Olympic leap starting from the bank and traveling up and out, higher than anyone, arms twirling and legs jerking, face lit up like fireworks, and then, just at the moment his first toe touched, a cry so loud and clear as to be heard for miles. What we all heard that night, the last night anything would be all right, was Andrew crying out his happiness, his one word that meant everything that mattered to him, his one word replacement for everything he had already lost: *Delia!"*

I look up and finish my story, "He never came back up. He drowned."

"It's bullshit," the psychiatrist said.

"Bullshit? I couldn't save him. How is it bullshit?"

"First, no one records memory in this way. Too artsy. Sorry. Too *literary.* Who do you think you're talking to? This isn't a reading."

"Second?" I asked.

"Second, I don't believe you."

"Why?"

"Because you speak for the other people as if you could read their minds. How in the hell could you know that 'swimming at night' is the only thing that could 'induce such freedom' for Andrew, much less Fiona and Delia."

"I said it was dream."

"And do you possess ESP in your dreams?"

"No, I just know things," I said. "You know. In the dream."

"It's a song," he says.

"What song?"

"It's by REM. The song is called 'Night Swimming.' I have the disc at home."

"I have it too. It used to belong to Andrew."

"Of course you have it. You're quoting lines word for word. *Recklessness and water.* Who says that?"

"I just did. I even added a little haunting waver to my voice."

"But it's not *your* voice. Michael Stipe is the singer."

"Just then it was mine."

"And what about those names. Are they fake? Who do you know named Fiona and Delia anymore?"

"Delia is real."

"And Fiona?"

"Sally."

"Right. Sally." The psychiatrist laughed quietly under his breath. "From now on, spare me the lyrical prose and plagiarism. Tell me what happened. You know, *the plot.* How did Andrew die?"

"I told you he drowned," I said.

"He didn't drown. He died of cancer. I read it in the obits. Hodgkin's disease followed quickly by a virus in his heart."

"It's the same."

"How is it the same?" the psychiatrist asked.

"He's dead," I answered. "How is it different?"

Session 2

"In the morning, Fiona and I slept through the alarm and breakfast and work and finally woke at noon. Fiona smiled, pulling on jeans and T-shirt and cowboy boots.

The water's not too cold in here, I said. *The water is not cold.*

You'll be fired, she said.

You'll flunk summer school.

Good, she said. *I love to fail.*

The water is warm.

"And so Fiona stripped out of her cowboy boots and jeans and T-shirt and climbed back into bed."

"Good grief," the psychiatrist said. "First, I don't know why you are telling me this. Second, when you run dialogue, I can never keep up with who is saying what."

"If this were written down, you could see the quotation marks and line breaks. Or in this case, italics."

"Why italics?"

"To separate what I am saying to you from what the characters are saying to each other."

"Any why, pray tell, are *we* a part of the story?" the psychiatrist asked. "You can put that 'we' in italics if you like. For emphasis."

"The involvement of a writer with his psychiatrist is always present in the work," I said. "So why not bring it to the page."

"I'll tell you why. Because people like to read stories. Not stories within stories. And certainly not the metanarrative crap you seem to be blabbing on about. Anyway, you told me it was a dream."

"I changed my mind. It's not a dream. It's real. But back to your point about metanarrative fiction. If the writer wants to tell the story of a friend's death, for example, and is not able to do it on his own because he has created a mental break from the death and therefore seeks therapy as a means to getting at the truth, isn't it more honest to include the psychiatrist in the story? Metanarrative or not, it's more honest."

"So you acknowledge the mental break, this drowning—this fiction—and yet cannot part with it."

"It's like this. If Andrew died of cancer, it can't be my fault. I mean maybe I could have put lead paint chips in his cereal or something, but no one would believe that. Unfortunately, I'm a really nice guy. Everyone says so. But a drowning. Something I could have prevented, but didn't act fast enough. Maybe I froze with fear and watched him die. They'll hate me for it."

"And you want them, whoever they are, to hate you?" the psychiatrist asked.

"Of course."

"Explain."

"How can I be a tragic figure if it's not my fault? *They* are my audience. *They* need a tragic figure. *They* demand it."

Session 3

"Last time, you told me about having sex with Fiona the morning after the accident. Why?"

"It lends itself to how callous and inappropriate I am."

"Ahh. The joke about warm water."

"Exactly."

"But why does Fiona go along with the joke?"

"I figure she should be callous too."

"It's really not callousness. It makes you both psychopaths. Is that what you want? If it is, I'd go with paint chips in the cereal. But you should know they don't cause cancer, they make you retarded."

"Well. Strike the sex. I'll revise my ending to the drowning so that the reader gets to see me not save Andrew. Or maybe they'll see me not save myself. I'm not sure yet."

"That won't make them hate you. That will make them sympathize with you and pity you for beating yourself up. Or they'll think you're crazy," the psychiatrist said. "I think you want them to pity you."

"Maybe a little, I said. "He was my best friend."

"Ah ha! This is good. Say more about this."

"You sound cliché when you say things like that."

"You could pencil me in a more eloquent psychiatrist? You could make me feisty. More of a loose cannon, really. A cowboy shrink."

"Only if you help me sort out this death."

"Then tell me what really happened. Is there a plot to this story?"

"No plot."

"You may very well be the worst writer ever," the psychiatrist said.

"Plot is dead. No one reads for plot anymore."

"Oh yes they do. People love plot. *They* demand it. Maybe not literary snobs and second-rate writers, but everyone else. If we don't have plot, we quit reading."

"What about right now, at this very moment? In order for this story to be alive, to exist, then someone's eyes are on the page right now. Some one, as we speak, is reading these words, without plot."

"They are reading to find out what really happened to Andrew."

"No," I say. "You already told them about the cancer. They know how he died. They are reading to find out what it means to me."

"Who gives a shit about that?"

"Well you damn well better, I'm paying you enough."

"Ah ha! Now we're getting somewhere."

"Where?"

"Money," the psychiatrist said.

"What?"

"Everything is about money. Sex, really, but money too."

"I might make money off this story? Is that what you mean?"

"You'll turn your best-friend-died-pity-party into quick cash. *The New Yorker* loves a good cancer story."

"Quick cash? The New Yorker? Do you know *anything* about writing?"

"I know you're writing about me so you won't have to write about your best friend's death. I know you blame yourself for his death. I know you are smart enough to recognize how irrational this is, but continue to do so anyway. What I don't know is *why?*"

Session 4

"Andrew landed in the water. He flailed around and we all laughed, not knowing he was drowning. We'd been drinking and smoking pot, and maybe we thought everything could be a joke. I swam to him after he stopped flailing. I dove under and grabbed his arm, so pale and thin. I pulled him to the bank and started CPR. I only vaguely remembered what to do. Fiona and Delia tried too. He didn't respond."

"And the cancer." The psychiatrist tipped back his Stetson and fingered his new moustache.

"The same," I said. "I sat at his bedside, thinking it had to be some kind of joke, that if I waited a little longer, he'd sit upright and laugh at me. He'd point his bony fingers and say how stupid I looked. But before I knew it, they were saying the virus was in his heart. They were saying they couldn't do chemo because of the virus. They said they couldn't treat the virus for the Hodgkin's. They said they would have to take him off the breathing machine and let him go. So they did."

"You think these two stories are the same?"

"Exactly the same."

"And what about Fiona and Delia. Why are they in the story?"

"They lend credibility to the drowning. Witnesses. And they allow for the possibility of sex. Readers like that."

"Couldn't there be sex between you and Andrew?" The psychiatrist pulled on the ends of his bolo tie. "I've seen *Brokeback Mountain* four times."

"I guess, but that sort of creeps me out. My relationship with Andrew wasn't like that. I loved him in other ways."

"But he didn't really drown and you tell people that? How do you decide where to lie and where to be honest?"

"I see your point."

"Of course you do, you're the one writing this."

"That's true," I said.

"Where is all this going anyway?"

"Maybe I'll send it off to a little magazine somewhere. It could be a story for Andrew. It could have a dedication and everything."

"Sounds lame to me."

"Well I already gave money to the library for that ridiculous stained glass window. This is more personal. It could be a song."

"A song?" The psychiatrist stood up and crooned, "Git along, little doggies!"

"Do you even know what that means?"

"No idea." The psychiatrist sat back down. "And these boots are killing me."

"I'm talking about 'Night Swimming.' That REM song. It's what was playing in my car when I left the hospital."

"And so you recreated his death through the song."

"Something like that."

"The reality didn't allow you to feel the way you thought you should, so you invented a new death. You superimposed the events of the song onto your own life. The life of a fiction writer. You then combined all three things: the death, the song, and the writing. You tried to create something new. Something you could live with."

"You're finally starting to sound like a psychiatrist," I said.

"I still think you're the worst writer ever."

"Then I'll write you out of the story."

At which point the psychiatrist stood up and took off his hat. He walked out of the office. He took the elevator to the ground floor and made his way across the lobby. Outside, he jogged across the street and down the grassy slope to the lake at the center of the office park. He did not stop jogging until the water reached his waist. Then he lurched forward. He jerked and twisted to the center of the lake in his suit and bolo tie and brand new cowboy boots. Then he let out his breath and slipped underwater, sinking fast, for he was muscular man with dense structure. He did not know how to swim. And when he began to convulse, he appeared comic, grabbing the water and popping up and down. With very little surprise, the psychiatrist drowned.

I watched it happen.

Afterwards, I got into my car. I did not call the police or an ambulance. I did not mourn his death. I did not blame myself. No one would miss such a lousy shrink. No one would miss his moustache or stupid hat. I would not. I would not miss anyone, ever again. I pulled a knife from the glove box and cut a deep hole in my chest. While driving, I reached in and cut love out and threw it from the window. Love sat bloody on the side of the road, a carcass to be gigged by prisoners in orange jumpsuits and shoved into plastic bags. On the car stereo, REM played "Night Swimming." Michael Stipe crooned on about *recklessness and water.* He sang it with that haunting waver in his voice. *His* voice. Not mine.

And for the first time, the song did not involve me.

CAB RIDE

Leaving Miami airport, Camille and I hail a cab driven by a very small man with skin the color of oiled mahogany. He looks to stand five feet tall. We've flown Blue in, and to our surprise, he greets the dog first. The man scratches behind Blue's ears and says, *Jambo! Hujambo, Toto.* We lift our bags into the trunk while the man nods and smiles at Blue. He opens the front door and Blue hops in. Camille and I take the back. Inside, the cab smells like Old Spice and pine needles. The man's ID card reads: Casimiri Kapinga.

Camille takes a guess and says, "Jambo."

Casimiri cranes his neck, "Yes, hello! Where you go today?"

"Econolodge," I say. "Jambo."

He offers a genuine smile and nods as he turns back to face the road. He reaches across the seat and massages Blue's shoulders.

"Good dog," he says.

"Very good," Camille says. "Do you have a dog?"

"No. I have," Casimiri pauses. He holds his hands up, ten inches apart. "Paka. Paka. Eh, cat!"

"What's his name?" I ask.

"Name is Usiku," he says. "Usiku mean night."

"Usiku," Camille says. "She's a black cat."

139

"Yes," he says. "All over."

As we reach the last section of outdoor airport parking, Casimiri stops the cab. A pickup truck filled with mountain bikes reverses into the exit. The driver wants to back in and claim the last parking place in the lot. Casimiri doesn't seem to understand this and has pulled within inches of the truck's bumper. The driver of the pickup is white and shirtless and bald. Both nipples are pierced. He jumps out and motions for the cab to back up. Casimiri still doesn't understand.

"I have right-of-way," he says.

Another shirtless biker approaches the cab. All the windows are down. This biker looks to have been waiting on the pickup truck for his friends and his bike.

He says, "What the fuck is wrong with you, nigger? Back that shit up."

Casimiri says, "You move, we exit."

"We can't do nuthin until you move this cab. Stupid nigger, go back to your country. Start swimmin', man."

The driver of the pickup continues to motion for the cab to back up with his hands. His shaved head gleams in the sun. Casimiri looks left, then right. Then he raises as much of his tiny body out of the window as possible.

He crunches up his brow and shouts, "Is this how it be? Is this how it be in you country? *Nenda kutomba!*"

Camille and I slouch down low in our seats. Blue begins to growl.

"Easy, Blue," I say.

"I thought we were past this in the South," she says.

"We're not in the South," I say. "We're in Miami."

The biker steps closer. He stands six feet from the window and I decide he can't be more than sixteen. He's got a tattoo on his pale muscled chest that says *Ride Hard*. Camille turns her ring, still unsized and loose, such that the diamond faces her palm. The biker takes another step and cuts six feet to three.

He tugs on the button of his cut-off jeans and says, "How about you suck my cock, you little nigger. Just back yer fucking cab up. We ain't going nowhere 'til you back this shit up."

He continues to slide his waistband up and down and side to side. Blue barks and growls. Camille grabs his collar with one hand and squeezes my arm with the other.

Casimiri says, "So this is how it be. So this is how it be in you country. You the nigger, you a *baiskeli kuma. Mama yako ananyonya mboo ya farasi!*"

Then Casimiri sighs and backs up the cab a few feet. The pickup maneuvers into the free space. We squeal through the exit with Casimiri, the biker, and the pickup driver all flipping the bird.

Six months ago, I dreamt that Camille lay next to me in bed. I told her I loved her, that I always had, and that I wanted to put things back together. In the dream, Camille had seven identical pink-skinned children and a wealthy husband, but was soon to be divorced. She would give up custody, all seven, to the immensely capable father. He brushed their blonde hair, all parts on the right, with manicured hands. Each child said, *Thank you, father,* with a smirk.

Camille lifted her chin and said, *I can't live here anymore. I should move back to the South. I don't belong here. I should move back to Alabama.*

So I said, *We should both go.*

Camille pulled her hair back and made a ponytail. Then she pulled the rubber band out and shook it free. *I don't know,* she said. *Things were bad last time. And I still won't have your son.*

In the dream, I smiled at her. I sat up and whistled for our dog, Blue, who jumped into the bed. *We've got Blue,* I said. *That's enough.* Camille drew her tongue across her lower

lip and said, *It's never enough. It never will be.* Then Camille's
face changed. She became Audrey, and then Heather. She
even became my mother, and then, for a startling instant,
she became me.

When I woke up, I poured a glass of scotch and wrote a
letter. A very long letter to Camille explaining all the reasons
she should forgive me. That I had already forgiven her. And
I threw it away.

So I poured another glass of scotch and wrote a different
letter. It looked exactly like this:

> *Dear Camille,*
> *How is Blue? I miss him. I miss you.*
> *Love, Ben*

I mailed that letter to an address I found on the internet.
San Francisco, California. In three weeks time, Camille wrote
back. The letter said only this: *I miss you too.* Beneath the
words, an actual paw print. The ink, of course, was blue.

Now out of the parking lot, Camille lets go of my arm. I
close my eyes.

Then she asks, "What's that last thing you said?"

"No no." Casimiri shakes his head. In the rearview mirror
I see that his eyes are dark as coal. "Very bad, what I say."

"Come on," she says. "You can tell us."

"Okay." He smiles and grips the steering wheel. "I say
his mum suck the horse's cock."

We all laugh and the spell is broken. I fill my lungs with air.

"How do you say 'dog' in your language?" I ask.

"Dog is *mbwa*"

"*Mmbawa?*" I say.

"*Mbwa*, yes." Casimiri says. "You stay in Miami?"

"No," Camille says, smiling. "We're driving to Key West
tomorrow. We're getting married."

"Very good, very good!" Casimiri smiles wide. He has beautiful teeth.

"We say in Kenya, *chanda chema huvikwa pete.*" Casimiri says. "A handsome finger get the ring."

We reach the hotel and I pay Casimiri. I give him a twenty dollar tip.

"I'm sorry," I say.

He nods, folding the money into his pocket.

"Have good sexy weekend," he says. Then he bends his knees and shakes his hips while singing the first line of Marvin Gaye's, "Let's Get it On."

Camille laughs and leans forward to high-five Casimiri. I watch him stare down her shirt. I wish I'd kept my money.

Then he opens the door for Blue and scratches behind his ears.

"Good dog," he says. "Good dog."

Blue wags his tail.

JIMBO THAMES

You should know about Jimbo Thames. He was tall and skinny with wiry blonde hair and a nose like a hawk's beak. He was tough too. One night we sat in Donna Pike's parents' kitchen and traded punches to the gut. We quit after three each. Jimbo said that when he played with Donna's brother David, he wouldn't quit until he spat up blood on the countertop. We both admired him for that.

Then Jimbo pulled a sheet of acid from the freezer. He said it keeps better in there. He told Donna's mom it was a fruit roll up and that he liked them cold. Jimbo told me that she said, *I've never seen them with the little bears drawn on it. Where can I buy those?* We laughed hard. Then Jimbo put a tab on my fingertip. He put one on his own fingertip and pressed it against his tongue.

"Like this," he said.

"Are you sure?"

"Come on, man. It's not every day we get our hands on good stuff."

I touched my finger to my tongue. It didn't taste like anything. Maybe a little like glue, but I'd been drinking for hours and couldn't be sure.

"Okay. I'm ready," I said.

"Chill. It'll take a while. I'm gonna double up."

Jimbo put another tab on his tongue, right next to the

first one. He rolled his eyes and pretended to choke. I drank from my beer.

"Dude," Jimbo said. "You have to wait until it absorbs. You fucked it up."

"But it's in me, right?"

"I don't know. You're just not supposed to take it off your tongue until it absorbs."

"Fuck it," I said.

"I'm gonna triple up."

"You're a crazy motherfucker."

But then he did it. I watched him. He put that third hit of acid right on his tongue. Three squares of colored paper making a little triangle. I'd never seen acid before. And I even spit mine out while Jimbo wasn't looking. I stuck it on my shoe.

Donna walked in wearing a party hat. She put a red bow into her deep cut V-neck and laughed.

"Can I be a birthday present on my own birthday?" she said.

Then she grabbed my hand.

I was having sex for the first time when the train severed Jimbo's arm. Donna took her shirt off before we even closed the door to her parent's bedroom. She pushed me flat against the bed and straddled me with her skirt hiked up. Neither one of us said anything about birth control.

"This is what I want," she said. "I'm sixteen now."

"I'm fifteen," I said.

She took off my clothes at the same time Jimbo took off his. He had run through the Alabama woods naked, screaming and jumping. He picked up a thick chunk of pine and beat the ground the way his father beat him. The way my father beat me. I imagine it's the way I might have beaten you, if I'd had the chance. Jimbo ran to the railroad tracks and lay down. He cried.

When the train arrived, Jimbo might not have known what it was. We won't ever know the truth. Maybe he knew exactly what was coming. Maybe he knew it was the westbound Amtrak Sunset Limited. All we know for sure is that he must have made a last minute attempt to get out of the way. He only lost his arm. But it was dark and the train was loud and no one heard him scream. They say the conductor might have been drinking, or sleeping, or both. The train never stopped.

Jimbo Thames bled to death while Donna bounced up and down on me in her parents' bed. Jimbo bled to death while David walked in on us just after and gave me a black eye. He bled to death while Donna screamed at him for being such an asshole. He bled to death while I went back into the kitchen for a bag of frozen peas and a beer.

Jimbo Thames bled to death. That's where the story always ends. Except for this one time. This time I want to say, at least you didn't die like that. At least you didn't lie screaming in your own blood, armless, inches from the noise and smoke of a barreling train. But then I think about how you died, and how it really might not have been that much different. Donna wouldn't tell me.

For all I know, it was exactly the same.

RACE DAY

The old Mercedes hammers down the highway at ninety miles an hour. The sun hangs above receding Rocky Mountains and a burning orange light fills the car. East of Santa Fe, the land goes flat. The back seat holds Madison's duffle bag, rain coat, three hanging shirts, one case of beer, and an atlas. A cooler sits in the passenger seat. Empty beer bottles clink in a few inches of cold water. He scans radio stations for the news, but raspy static jostles through the speakers. He settles on NASCAR for the good reception. As Texas scrolls by, he learns that Jeff Gordon and Dale Earnhardt Junior are rivals. He learns that Dale Earnhardt Senior has been killed in the Daytona 500 three years ago, and that fans hope Junior might win on race day tomorrow. The odds look good. He learns expressions like *tattoo his bumper* and *swappin' paint*, and marvels at the hazards of life on the track.

Madison keeps a bottle of bourbon between his legs and makes a game of taking a shot at every state line. Louisiana, Mississippi, Alabama. Not much of a game. Madison decides to take a shot at every used car lot. He adds Burger Kings and drive-thru liquor stores. Dropping down to I-10 East, he spots a billboard with a smiling oyster that says, *Fried, Stewed, or Nude!* The oyster's arms and legs seem to dance in a fiery black iron skillet. For that one, Madison drinks twice.

Madison makes the cabin before sunrise. He's drunk, but it's a controlled drunk. Not the sort of drunk he intends to find soon. Just the same, he shudders, standing in a pool of Alabama moonlight some 3,000 miles from home. He stayed in this very cabin a few times as a child, but nothing seems familiar. The owner had told him the key would be under the mat on the back porch, and it is, so he lets himself in. The door has been hung backwards, opening out to the porch. Inside, the heat is crushing. Madison finds the light switch and flicks a dingy yellow glow across the room. He drops his bags inside the door, pries off clay covered wingtips and sets the new key on an oak and iron coffee table. He scans the spartanly furnished den and heads for the kitchen. A long, open bar separates the two rooms. The appliances look like they work and the water he cups and sips from the sink tastes fine.

The bedroom sits adjacent to the den and Madison rocks on the bed, testing the firmness. He retrieves a small, framed picture from his bag and holds it in his hands. In the photograph, a young boy sprints on a blacktop running track. His arms pump and his legs bulge with muscle. The blue uniform tank top darkens with sweat. The boy's veins pop taut across his forearms and neck, and his eyes squint down deep under a low brow. Madison places the photograph on the bedside table next to the phone, picks up the receiver, and sets it back down. A largemouth bass gapes at him from the wall. A red button stands out against the faux-wood plaque. He pushes the button. The fish begins to flip flop and sing Al Green's "Take Me to the River." Madison gulps from the bottle.

Still awake at sunrise, Madison walks onto the back porch. He lights a cigarette and looks out over the lake. Dead cypress trees rise from the rippled water. Spanish moss hangs limp from the branches. The greens of loblolly pines, asparagus fern, and sweet gum fleck the edges of the lake, and here beside the cabin, it's Eastern hemlock. To the far left, he can just make out the edge of the owner's house. Joan and Gideon Lester. He watches an alligator's head glides across the far side of the lake. He guesses ten inches from eyes to nose. Then he changes inches to feet. It's a trick his father taught him. He knows that beneath the surface swims a half-ton animal, ten-feet long with devil's horns running the length of his back. Madison wonders if the Lester's have small children. He tears off a sprig of hemlock and smells it. Returning inside, he removes the bottom shelf from the fridge and slides in his beer. He pulls a half dozen bottles of bourbon from a bag, fifths of Wild Turkey, and steps into the kitchen to hunt for a glass.

Madison finds two Dale Earnhardt commemorative glasses in a cabinet and holds one up to the light. He smiles for knowing who it is. The glass looks clean enough, but he wipes it with a dishrag just the same. Madison fills half the glass. He grabs a few ice cubes from the freezer and drops them in, ticking and popping in the bourbon. He realizes the kitchen doesn't have a dishwasher. He's always had one, except for when he was a child. That was sixty years ago, right here in Barlo. That was before his mother moved them to New England, before the money ran out, and before Gideon's father started buying up the land, acre by acre. He is alone now and a dishwasher won't matter. There will be no guests. After finishing and refilling the glass, Madison walks into the bedroom and sits on the bed. He stares at the picture on the bedside table. Picking up the phone, he pauses at the sound of his own breath in the ear piece. He returns it to the cradle. His back aches from the drive, so he pulls his legs up onto the bed, fetal. He stares at the ceiling until he can see the Daytona 500, four dozen numbered cars scorching across the roof beams in a mirage of heat.

"Gordon's ridin loose, Junior's ridin tight," Madison slurs. "It's anyone's game."

Then he passes out.

Waking to early afternoon, Madison puts on coffee and starts the shower. The water is slow to heat, and he glares into the mirror while he waits. Over the past year, his hair turned completely white, even the eyebrows. Madison's chest slopes inward as if he'd lain down and a cue ball had been dropped from a great height. Yellowing skin sags beneath his eyes. He showers, shaves, and puts the full amount of the first month's rent, all cash, into an envelope. The cabin doesn't deserve this much money, but it's the only way Gideon would agree to rent the place from month to month. Madison pulls on a new pair of jeans and is surprised to find them so stiff and uncomfortable. His suit felt better than this. The new flannel shirt makes him sweat. He takes it off and grabs his white button down. It stinks of bourbon. But here in this stretch of piney woods and buggy swamp, it couldn't matter less.

He pours a jigger of Wild Turkey into his coffee and starts driving toward the Lester house. Madison isn't sure how to get there, but he hopes that by following the dirt roads close to the lake, he'll eventually find it. It isn't long before he drives aimlessly through pine stands and grassy fields, red dust curling up from behind his Mercedes in wide, hazy clouds. After an hour, sweat bleeds through his clothes and he's made three U-turns.

"These red roads," he says. "These red fucking roads!" Madison pops his palm against the steering wheel. He hasn't shouted in days, maybe months, and the sound of it shocks him.

About fifty yards ahead, he can just make out a sign. Driven deep into the ground at a three-way intersection, the sign is barely visible through the high grass. Madison stops and pulls a pint of bourbon from the cracked mahogany-paneled glove compartment. The sign reads *Mt. Erebus Church* in faded black stenciling on plywood, accompanied by a crude arrow pointing up one of the roads. Madison wipes sweat from his forehead with a handkerchief and takes a gulp from the bottle. He tosses both into the passenger seat. Grass stands two-feet high in the center of the ascending road, and only thin ruts of red clay show through. He turns up the drive. The tall grass flutters under the dirty dented fenders of the Mercedes. At the top of the rise, the road takes another sharp right and passes through an open gate. The vertical posts of the gate climb four feet higher than the makeshift fence. Rusty nails hold bleach-white antlers to every inch of wood and a cattle ditch spans the width of the road. Madison sips his bourbon before crossing over.

Past the gate, the road widens and opens into a flower speckled field. Sunlight pours in through an unobstructed sky and a small white church appears against the regressing pines and poplar. The dull white church looks to be converted from an old barn. A shoddy steeple cut from an air duct teeters on the roof. The reflective surface gleams in the sun. A wooden cross, spray painted silver, is bound by wire to the top of the duct.

Under the shade of a loblolly pine, a little black boy draws lines in a sandbox: circles, zigzags, and spirals threaded out by a three pronged stick. Glass bottles suspended with fishing line hang from the branches of the pine. A hundred of them turn in the wind. From Coke bottles to glass salt shakers—all clear—the bottles gape lidless, cooing above the boy. Madison pulls himself up from the low coupe. He takes another snort of bourbon and throws the empty pint bottle to the ground. He slams the door. The little boy looks up from the sand and points his stick at Madison.

"Hiya there." Madison puts on a big smile and waves.

"Anyone else around? Maybe inside?" Madison points at the church as he approaches. The boy, drooling now, stares at him, still pointing with his stick.

"Hey, looks good," Madison says. "Sort of like little rainbows." He stoops down and examines the sand drawings. He looks over to the boy. The boy holds a severed rooster foot, tight in his undersized hands. Madison takes a step back. The boy waves the clawed foot at Madison, a yo-yo of shaking slobber lolling from his cracked, pink lips.

"Jesus," Madison says.

"Ump," the boy says, pointing to his forehead with a free hand.

"Well all right," Madison says.

A thin white man with long tangles of dirty blonde hair steps out from the church's sliding barn door.

"I see you found Jesus," he says. The man's oversized, black button-down has been worn to the point of sun-bleached shoulders. Black jeans bleed into black boots. He seems to march in place on the concrete slab extending from the door.

"Jesus?" Madison asks.

"Jesus," the man says. He stops marching and looks out into the woods.

"What?"

"I said Jesus." The man pauses, scratches his stubble. "Jesus is the Reverend's boy."

"This kid's name is Jesus?"

"You been drinkin?"

"What?" Madison squints in the sun. "No."

"Yeah, the boy's name is Jesus."

"Oh." Madison shades his eyes with his hand and looks at the man, then the boy. Jesus stares at Madison.

"I've gotten a little turned around on all these clay roads." Madison forces a smile.

"I see that."

The boy points the foot at Madison.

"You got a lazy eye," the man says.

"Yeah," Madison says.

"Jesus don't like it none." The man shakes his head side to side. "You born with it?"

"The condition developed when I was nine."

"That's peculiar."

"So they tell me," Madison says. "Listen, I could really use some directions."

"I imagine," the man says. "Come on then." He turns to the church door and mutters something under his breath. He marches in place, four false steps, then walks inside.

The church is like nothing Madison has ever seen. Instead of pews, picnic tables. Instead of columns, PVC pipe painted silver. Instead of an altar, two pine workhorses support a plywood table top draped in thin white sheets. Careful hands have stenciled *The Face of God* onto the fabric. On top of the altar, a large crown sits next to an oversized, leather-bound book. Intricate patterns of white beads and silver sequins decorate the crown. A large quartz crystal crests the center. Madison's eyes move from the crown to a row of aquariums sidling the left aisle. Canebrake rattlers, timber rattlers, southern copperheads, and water moccasins twist and hiss in the glass tanks. They slither up the sides of the glass and dart splayed tongues through mesh lids.

The tall thin man watches Madison watch the snakes. He scratches his stubble. He marches in place. Then, as if told to do so, he cries out: "In His name, they shall be castin' out devils!"

Madison closes his eyes and arches his brow, "Jesus Christ."

Red-faced, the man continues, "They shall speak with new tongues. They shall be taking up the serpents! And if they drink a deadly thing, it shall not hurt them!"

The man rolls up one sleeve and reaches into a glass tank.

He pulls out a four-foot canebrake rattler. The yellow-gray snake writhes in his hand, oily black bands encircling its thick body. When the thin man lifts it up, the serpent promptly sinks a pair of fangs deep into his thumb. He screams with tremendous volume and throws the snake to the ground. Madison, not normally athletically inclined, leaps to the top of the nearest picnic table in scissor-kick fashion. The rattler, frantically hissing and striking, slips out the open door.

"Rob-Rob," a voice says.

A tall black man with dreadlocks and beard enters from the back.

"Rob-Rob!" he shouts.

Rob-Rob clutches his thumb at his stomach. His eyes bulge.

"Never handle the snakes before they've been fed." The man grabs Rob-Rob's hand and examines his swollen thumb. It's twice normal size.

"I could drive him to a hospital," Madison says.

"No," the man says. He pushes up billowing white sleeves. Black hand-stitched symbols decorate the shirt.

"But he needs a doctor."

"We here at Mt. Erebus have our own ways. We have faith." The man raises his eyes to the barn rafters. "And if they drink any deadly thing, it shall not hurt them."

"Seriously?" Madison asks.

"Rev, I feel sick," Rob-Rob says. "I just held him up. Like you do in service. I did what you did."

"Excuse us," the Reverend says. He leads Rob-Rob to the back of the church. Rob-Rob fights the Reverend at the door, attempting to march in place. Then he freezes; all color leaves his face. As the Reverend guides him through the door, Rob-Rob vomits down his chest.

Madison walks out the front and lights a cigarette. It takes him three tries to strike the match. He looks to the sandbox, but Jesus is gone. The wind picks up and suspended bottles whistle and coo, swaying in the pine. The sun refracts off edges and screw tops, white light and rainbows jumping from needle to branch.

Madison walks to his car and opens the trunk. Inside, he pulls a liter of Wild Turkey from the spare tire well. He lifts the bottle to his lips and forces down the hot bourbon. It burns in his throat and his hands continue to shake. Madison gets back in the Mercedes. He still doesn't have directions. Something taps at his window and Madison turns to find rooster claws scratching the glass.

"Jesus!" Madison shrieks.

"Wuh," the boy says. Jesus stares through dull white pupils.

"No. I mean, I meant..." Madison stops and rests his forehead on the steering wheel.

"Sorry, Jesus. Run along now." He laughs a little as he starts up the coupe. He says it again: "Run along now, Jesus." Madison pulls away from Jesus and drives back onto the red clay. As he accelerates to the antler-covered gate, a loud pop sounds from the Mercedes. The engine grinds, shakes, and dies. The car rolls to a stop on the first bar of the cattle grate.

Madison slams both fists against the steering wheel and sinks down in his seat. He takes the Wild Turkey from between his legs and drinks until he gags. He gets out and looks under the hood. This is no different from any other time Madison has peered at an engine. The hoses, clamps, belts, and wires mean nothing, boozy vision or not. Madison pulls out the dipstick and looks vacantly at the oily tip. It's the only mechanical thing he knows about cars, but even with this, he isn't sure. He throws it into the woods. Jesus stands at a distance, staring.

"What the hell is wrong with you?" Madison calls out.

Jesus turns and scuttles to the church. His knees don't fully extend and he compensates by lunging his upper body forward with each stride.

He tries the ignition again. The car shakes and grinds, but doesn't start. Madison slumps down and sips a little bourbon. He dials up NASCAR on the radio: *Look at 'em go! Gordon and Junior swapping paint out of the turn. Good gosh it's going to be close!*

"Come on, Junior," Madison says. "Beat Gordon's ass. Make your daddy proud."

Madison closes his eyes.

"Looks like you got a busted belt," a voice says from behind the raised hood.

Madison sits up, awake. An hour has passed.

"What?" he says.

"Busted belt," the voice says. "And I'd bet you need more oil, but I can't find your dipstick." Dreadlocks appear from behind the hood and the Reverend walks up to the open window.

"I've got some oil out in the shed," the Reverend says.

"What the hell," Madison says. "What are you doing to my car?"

"Fixing it."

"How do I know that."

"You're blocking the gate. I need this shit-heap out of here."

"Hey there, nigger, this is a Mercedes."

"Maybe in the eighties. Now it's a shit-heap. And as for what you called me, this ain't the land of cotton."

"That's a shame."

Madison climbs out of the coupe and shades his eyes. He tries to take a deep breath but his lungs feel as if they've collapsed. The reverend walks toward a large shed and Madison jogs a few clumsy, aching steps to catch him.

"Can you really fix it?" Madison asks.

"I doubt it," the Reverend says. "But I can tow you out."

"I need to find my landlord's house. To pay the rent. Right now I'd just as soon go home."

"I guess you rented the Lester cabin."

"How'd you know?"

"Not much else around here. Mr. Lester owns everything in Barlo. He let us have these few acres for the church and the cemetery, since we'd already been here so long. But he's never come up to see it. The Lester family has been here four generations. We've been here longer than that."

The reverend tilts his head. "You look familiar."

"Can't see how."

"I'm Reverend Charon."

"Madison."

At the shed, the Reverend looks under tarps and scraps of wood. "Even if I find the oil, I know I don't have a belt."

"I wouldn't know what to do with it if you did." Madison wipes the sweat off his forehead.

"I could swear I know your face."

"Not unless you've been out west."

"I spent a few years in Hattiesburg."

"I was a bit further west than that."

"Here's the oil," he says, still looking. "No belt." Then he lifts a set of keys from a nail. "I guess I'll be taking you home."

The Reverend drives an old pick-up truck out from behind the shed. Madison gets in the Mercedes and sets the gear shift to neutral. The Reverend eases the pick-up to the rear bumper of the car. Then he over accelerates and rams the Mercedes before pushing it through the gate. Madison spills booze in his lap. He flips the bird through his back window and the Reverend smiles. On the other side of the gate, he drives around the Mercedes and reverses to the front bumper. Each man ties one end of a length of rope to their vehicle.

"Why are you helping me?" Madison asks.

"I'm not helping you," the Reverend says. "I'm just moving you along."

In tow, Madison sits in his coupe and drinks from the bottle. He steers now and then as the Reverend makes turns or takes sharp curves. He can barely see for the clouds of dust and mostly watches shadows of pine trees blinking at the windows. They pass a cemetery and Madison swears he can see faces on the gravestones. Not just etchings, but three dimensional faces pushing out into the sun. He drinks from the bottle.

He finds NASCAR on the radio and listens to the Daytona 500: *The track here is 2.5 miles long and the curves are banked at 31 degrees. These guys are knocking out 200 laps in blistering 120-degree heat. Some drivers wear a cool-suit with capillary tubes woven into the fabric. Cold water is pumped from an ice chest in the car through these tubes. Let me tell you, folks, it's hot in these cars.*

"It's sure hot in here," Madison says. He plays a new game by drinking whenever the commentator says the word *fast.* Then he adds the word *track.*

At the cabin, the Reverend unties the car and throws the rope in his truck bed. Madison stands beside the Mercedes and palms the hood for balance.

"You a NASCAR fan?" Madison asks.

"Here and there," the Reverend nods. "Daytona's today, right?"

"Yes, sir," Madison says. "I'm pulling for Junior."

"You and everybody." The Reverend pauses. "You got a junior somewhere?"

"Portland." Madison points at the sunset.

"That's a long way from here." The Reverend wipes his hands with a rag. "He know where you are?"

"Not for a long time now."

"I see."

"What about your boy?" Madison asks.

"What about him?"

"His eyes are white."

"Yeah, he's got the cancer. The white is tumors in his

pupils. He can see a little. Not much. They got a name for it, but I can't remember." The Reverend looks up at Madison. "Your eyes ain't quite right either."

"I know that," Madison says.

The Reverend nods and climbs back in the truck.

"Wait." Madison reaches into his pocket for the envelope of rent money. He slides out a fifty and holds it up.

"Here, thanks for the tow."

The Reverend laughs as he holds up the palms of both hands, shooing off the money.

"We'll settle up later," he says. "And don't worry, you don't need to pay your rent today. Mr. Lester won't do business on Sunday."

"Sunday. I guess it is."

"For some, it's a day of atonement." The Reverend pulls on his black beard.

"What the hell is that supposed to mean?"

But the Reverend has already started out the dirt drive, his dreadlocks masking any view of his face. He hangs an arm out the open window of the truck and flips Madison the bird. Madison nods. A hazy cloud of dust swirls in the air, settling red and dirty on the pine needle blanket covering the ground. Madison watches him until the truck is gone.

Inside, Madison throws his money and keys on the table. The cabin is hot. He turns on the shower and sits naked on the edge of the toilet. A low creak issues from the den and Madison raises his head from his hands. He doesn't hear anything else, but wraps on a towel and peers out the bathroom door. Nothing seems amiss, so he walks through the bedroom to the den. Out of the corner of his eye, Madison thinks he sees a shadow flit across the window, but he turns to find nothing. He blames his lazy eye. After the shower, Madison drapes on a robe and steps into the kitchen. There are no groceries. He finds a jar of pickles in the fridge and eats one with a beer. The dill turns his stomach so he puts them back. He makes a tall bourbon and water and returns to the den. He lights a cigarette, sits on the couch, and gulps his drink. He turns on the TV and flips to NASCAR.

Outside, Rob-Rob pours gasoline onto the sides of the cabin. He methodically makes his way around, one wall at a time. At the front and back doors, he wedges a two-by-four between the doorknob and the ground and at last understands why he was told to hang them backwards. Reverend Charon crouches down with his son Jesus near the south wall. He holds a box of matches in his hands.

"Now look how I do it, Jesus," the Reverend says. "I hold the match like this, and I slide it fast against the box."

"Ump," Jesus says. "Fah Fah."

"Watch me now," the Reverend says. He strikes the match.

Inside, Madison refills his glass. He pounds his fist on the coffee table.

"Come on, Junior!" he shouts.

On TV, Gordon leads Junior by a car length. The commentator breaks in: *Junior's drawin' in on Gordon. Looks like he's going the distance.*

"There it is, Junior." Madison says. "Hammer that son of a bitch."

Junior knows just how much bumper to give, the commentator says. *He can push Gordon's car where he wants without spinning him.*

"You got it, Junior," Madison says. "Put a tattoo on his bumper!"

Junior's dipping to the inside...he's within a foot of Gordon at 190 miles per hour...He's comin' up fast! Ya'll don't blink, this is it!

"That's right, Junior!" Madison shouts. "You know your daddy's watching."

He drains a fresh drink and stands up to scream at the TV.

Outside, the Reverend puts a match into Jesus' right hand and the box into the other. He holds Jesus' hands inside his own and makes the motions of striking a match. "See how easy it is?" the Reverend says. "Do it like this. You've earned it."

Jesus moves his right hand in spastic jerks. He misses the box by several inches. The Reverend eases the match and the box closer together and guides Jesus' hands. By now Rob-Rob has completed his circle of the house and pours the last of the gasoline into a pool on the ground. Rob-Rob looks to Jesus and smiles. In moonlight, Rob-Rob's face is pale like a ghost. He scratches his stubble and marches in place.

They can hear Madison screaming inside the cabin as Dale Earnhardt Junior wins the Daytona 500. Madison howls and stomps the floorboards.

"OK, Jesus," the Reverend says. "When we light this fire, it'll be big and bright like fireworks. And once it's going, it won't stop."

Jesus looks up to his father through sickly white pupils and smiles with excitement.

"All right, Jesus, let's light this match."

Directly across the lake, a ten-foot alligator crawls from her den. She lies on the sandbank and watches lights flicker inside the cabin. She watches blue shadows move beside it. Her brood of hatchlings wake and call to her with faint, throaty chirps. As she begins to ease herself backward into the den, a sudden flash of light expands and encircles the cabin. Crickets and tree frogs hush themselves. The mother alligator eyes the fire a moment longer. She listens as unnatural sounds and strange voices carry across the water.

She lifts her head, hissing at this new, arcane threat. Trees next to the cabin ignite and flames rise one-hundred feet into the night sky. She opens her jaws and bellows one tremendous growl, but the fire continues to grow.

The mother returns to her young.

VANILLA ORCHID

T he only thing Heather asks for when we move is a bed. Not a mattress set on skinny metal bars, but an honest-to-God bed with headboard and frame. She says a bed should be made from wood. She points to a magazine and says, *Sutter-style panel bed.* Then, *Crown molding, bun feet, mortis-and-tenon joinery.*

So I say, *I'll build it.*

I've got hands for wood and it's two months before I start a teaching job at Bayside Academy. Heather smiles. She knows I'm serious. We talked about this on our honeymoon at the Grand Hotel just three weeks ago. And I've done this before. I built our coffee table to the exact dimensions of a sushi service. I have my grandfather's lathe. I can handle this. I buy lumber, clear space in the garage, and dig my tools from moving boxes. I drop an old sheet to the floor and lug my work table to the center. I rip the picture from the magazine and tack it to the wall. The measurements are right here on the page.

I've got hands for wood. I can handle this.

My brother Graham stops by for coffee on Saturday. We're in the garage and I'm pointing out modifications to the bed.

"Look here," I say. I drop a finger on graph paper. "Drawers."

"Drawers?" he says.

"You'd never think to do it, would you? I could sink two drawers on each side. You know, sweaters, sheets, whatever."

"So what, you're going to dig holes in the mattress?"

"No. Come on. The mattress sits on top of beams."

Graham squints at the plans. "Won't that be sort of high?"

"A mattress is only ten-inches thick."

"But the box springs."

"Yeah. Those too. It won't be too high."

"You'll need a pole vault to get in bed."

"Fuck off."

"What about tools?"

"I'm all set. Pop's lathe, that jigsaw, and my baby here." I stroke the yellow handle of a circular saw. "It's a DeWalt. Heavy duty. Carbide-tipped blade."

"But you've got detail work in these plans."

"A few hand tools. That's all I need."

Graham pours the last of the coffee into his cup. The coffee maker turned up in the garage when we moved, and I've decided to keep it here for this project. For me, it's coffee all morning and Cokes in the afternoon. I don't sleep much, so caffeine keeps me moving. For a stretch in college, I felt lucky to get two straight hours. I wake at the faintest sound. If the ceiling fan hums at a higher pitch, I'm up. Heather is just the opposite. She'll sleep through lightning and thunder.

"Pop built this entire house," I say. "I can build a bed."

Graham sits on a stool and scratches stubble on his chin. He can grow a full beard in three days. He readjusts his baseball cap. We talk about the bed, the Grand Hotel, and Alabama's summer heat. Our mutt dog Blue circles twice, then lies at our feet. Graham finishes his coffee.

"Is Blue fixed?" Graham asks.

"They fix all the dogs at the pound," I say. "No exceptions."

"It's a shame. Blue is a fine dog."

"Blue was the best man in our wedding."

"So why don't you tell me why you really eloped."

"I just told you," I say. "Too much stress. Keep things simple. Two people, a waterfront view, a nice sunset. What more could you want?"

"Your family, for starters."

"I know. I know. But that's just not us. Heather and I wanted our day to be *our* day."

"Give me a fucking break. Weddings aren't about the bride and groom. It's the weepy mothers that deserve it. And hell, you've done this three times now."

"Uh huh. But don't forget the weepy stepmothers and half-sisters and that wanker third cousin who pissed in the azaleas and stole a bottle of bourbon from an open bar."

I sketch a circle into the headboard and look up. "Don't get me wrong, I had a great time at your wedding. But that's not what Heather wanted."

"Fine. But what about you?"

"I wanted the same thing. Just the two of us."

"No wankers."

"Not a one."

I tap my pencil on the work table and grin. Graham smiles back. Blue twitches oversized paws, chasing rabbits in his sleep.

"Can you believe we both moved back to Alabama?" I ask.

"My new job is worth it," he says. "But I didn't think you'd ever come back."

"And with Heather," I say. "That's the hardest part to believe."

"Sis won't come back," Graham says. "She wouldn't live in Alabama if they made her queen of Mardi Gras."

"She left because they *tried* to make her queen."

"Do you miss Virginia?" Graham asks.

"What's that supposed to mean?"

"Just what I said. I'm talking about the cabin, the dog, trout streams, cooler weather."

"Sure. The dog," I say. "I miss some things. But not others."

"Audrey wasn't all bad."

"But our relationship." I raise my eyebrows and exhale.

"Things looked good to me." Graham slips both arms inside his T-shirt and pushes out faux breasts. He stretches the shirt until it tears.

"You're an idiot," I say. "That's not even the right wife."

"I'm pretty sure that remembering who you were married to was *your* problem," he says. "At least you kept the dog this time."

Blue begins to bark. Not real barks, but quiet, dream barks that sound more like whimpers.

"My only child," I say.

"I should get back to little Ellie," he says.

"She's a sweet one."

"She is. You know she's shy of men now. Not sure why."

"Is that normal?"

"Sarah says it is. She's read all the books, so I'm sure it's fine. When are you guys going to step up?"

"Heather doesn't want kids. We've got Blue."

"You've said that."

"I'm with her."

"You'll come around. Both of you."

"We want what we want," I say.

"Yeah, yeah, yeah." Graham flicks a hand out and pats the air between us. He steps under the open garage door and into gauzy mist. "Better work on your bed, Ben. You can fill those drawers with rubbers."

When Heather wakes up, she rolls off our mattress and walks straight into the garage. She's in T-shirt and panties and her newly cropped hair stands on end. I can't get used to the haircut and I double-take when she steps into the light.

"Well?" she asks.

"It's been a week," I say. "I'm in the design phase."

"Just checking." Heather goes to the coffee pot. She picks it up, then puts it down.

"Graham stopped by. I'll make more."

"No. I'll make a pot in the kitchen. Your mother sent us a giant chrome thing that says it'll make a latte."

"Is that what that is?"

"It says it makes espresso. Steams the milk and everything. Push a button and presto, it's hot and ready."

I slip my hand between Heather's thighs.

"Presto," I say.

"Nope," she says. "I'm just hot."

I pull back my hand and shake it. I blow on my fingers.

"This humidity is unreal," I say.

"I'm sweating just standing here."

"Fairhope is hot," I say.

"Hot." Heather says this through a yawn. She lifts her arms and stretches her back, exposing a pink, dime-sized birthmark below her navel.

"I've been designing a carving for the headboard."

"A carving?"

"Yeah. An oak tree. Oaks symbolize love. I looked it up."

"Love." Heather raises her eyebrows and snorts.

"Love." I make a heart with my index fingers and thumbs. "If I add acorns, it could symbolize fertility, but I figure we'll be good with love."

"Are you shitting me with this?"

"No, ma'am. I am one artsy motherfucker."

Heather stands close and I wrap an arm around her waist. She still smells of salon chemicals. I kiss the nape of her neck. Her skin is damp with perspiration. The birthmark turns red.

A month later, we throw a dinner party. The boxes are gone, art hangs on the walls, and the to-do-list goes in the garbage. We have power, phone, cable, and water. Heather's Jeep and my Volvo carry Alabama plates, licenses, and insurance again. We've eaten two scoops of crawfish at Judge Roy Bean's and been out to see the Monday night movie at Red Bluff Theater. I even found a lake behind some soybean fields that I didn't know existed. There's a path through the woods and I can walk over without getting caught. When I'm frustrated by our bed, when the measurements don't match up, or when I ruin yet another *bun foot* on the lathe, Blue and I sneak out to the lake and fish.

But the house feels settled enough, so we invite three couples to dinner. Graham and Sarah, of course; they come early and help set up. Fred and Maxine arrive with a potted vanilla orchid. Heather swaps out her own centerpiece for the new one. Yellow flowers hang down like trumpets with softly curved openings. Long, thermometer-shaped buds dangle next to the blooms. Buds outnumber blooms four to one.

"Thank you so much," Heather says. "It looks like this will flower for weeks."

"We love them," Maxine says.

"Yeah," Fred says. "But get this. The flowers on these guys can only be pollinated in a single day. If the greenhouse man isn't there to hand-pollinate on that day, and just that *one* day, the vanilla bean won't form.

"This thing makes beans?" I ask.

"That makes me sad," Heather says. "How does it work in the wild?"

"I think there's a Mexican insect that does the dirty work," Fred says.

"The orchid pimp," Graham says, turning his hat sideways.

"Only one bottle of wine down and we've moved right into pimps," Maxine says. She lifts a glass of club soda on ice. "Cheers."

"Take your hat off," Sarah says. "This isn't fight night." Graham works a combination of upper-cuts in the air.

Shane and Delia let themselves in the front door, red-faced and carrying four bottles of wine. Blue barks and wags his thick brown tail. Shane lets Blue lick his face.

"Sorry we're late," Delia says. "Traffic."

"Sex," Shane says. He's got a thick red beard and perfect teeth.

"Pimps and sex," Sarah says. "Delightful."

Maxine and Sarah clink glasses.

"Welcome, welcome," I say. Heather and I take the wine bottles and put them on the sideboard.

"Wine, beer, or booze before dinner?" Heather asks.

"Two wines," Delia makes a peace sign with her hand and Shane grabs it. He bends down her middle finger. "One wine, one whisky."

Delia frowns and points her index finger at Shane. "Be good."

"Okay," I say. "Everybody knows everybody, right?"

"Maxine and Delia haven't met," Heather says, handing Delia her wine. I pour the scotch for Shane and hand it across the table.

"Maxine, Delia. Delia, Maxine," I say. Maxine stands a foot taller than Delia and when they shake hands, it looks as if Delia is in mid-curtsy.

"Shane, you remember Fred from Graham's wedding."

"You bet," Shane says. "Fred and I conspired to throw Graham in the Bay."

"Fuckers," Graham says. "I had to ride in the limo like that. They charged us extra. I got a rash in my crotch."

Shane and Fred high five.

"I love the house," Delia says. "Beautiful."

"We love it too," Heather says, then looks to me. "Just one last project and we're all set."

"It'll be done in three weeks," I say.

"What's all this?" Maxine asks.

"The pole-vault bed." Graham raises his glass.

"Shut up," I say. "It's going to be perfect."

"What, what, what?" Maxine says.

"Ben has decided to build a bed for us," Heather says. "Ben does great work. You've seen the coffee table."

"Sushi night!" Fred says. He squeezes his eyes shut and bows. Shane plays along and bows back.

"But this is a big project," Heather says.

"A bed should be rock solid," Shane says.

"It's fine," I say. "I've got it under control."

I turn to face the sideboard and pour fresh drinks.

After dinner, we step out onto the back porch so Shane can smoke. Blue runs into the yard and disappears into shadow. The Childress River slinks past, slow and bright with reflected moonlight.

"Why don't you ever fish the river?" Graham asks.

"I'm not sure anything's alive in there," I say. "Besides, I found a lake full of bluegill."

"Where?"

I look at my feet and whistle.

"Is it a fucking secret?" Graham asks.

As Shane lights his cigarette, Fred pulls out a handful of cigars.

"I've got a secret," Fred says.

"No you don't," Maxine says.

"Come on, Max, it'll be fine." Fred see-saws one cigar between his fingers. "Anyone join me?"

"Sure," I say. "What's the occasion?"

"Fred," Maxine says.

"Max here—" Fred begins.

"Fred." Maxine cuts him off and glares.

"We got one in the hopper!" With closed eyes, Fred lifts his chin up, bends his knees and thrusts his pelvis.

"Fred." Maxine crosses her arms. "We are *supposed* to wait until the doctors tell us it's safe."

Fred shrugs. Then he hands out cigars. Maxine and Sarah pass. As we light cigars and make toasts, I listen to Blue snuffling through the shrubs. He barks once, then growls, and something unseen scrambles over the fence. Blue stands on hind legs and sniffs the fencepost, a patch of light falling across his uneven ears.

"You know it's a miracle we're pregnant," Maxine says.

"Max," Fred says.

"What with Fred's, well, limitation." Maxine winks at Fred. Fred doesn't wink back.

"Give it up, Freddie," Graham says, lifting his fists.

"Slow swimmers?" Delia asks. "Cigars will do it."

"Raw oysters cancel those out," Shane says. "I eat them everyday."

"Thanks, Max," Fred says. His face goes slack. "I played rugby in college."

"Oh hell," I say. "I don't think I want to hear the rest of this."

"I do," Heather says.

Fred looks at his shoes. "We were in a pile up and a guy stomped my balls with his cleat."

We all groan.

"They removed one and fixed up the other. They said I'd function fine, but they didn't sound optimistic about fertility."

"Uniball," I say.

"Uniball hits a homerun," Graham adds.

"Freddie one nut," Shane says, extending a hand.

"Congratulations on your baby." They shake in earnest. Maxine giggles and pats a hand on her stomach.

"I can't believe you've kept this a secret all these years," Heather says.

"Would you tell that story?" Fred asks.

"I think it's sweet," Delia says. "One little ball triumphs over adversity."

At this, everyone laughs. Shane squeezes Delia and kisses the top of her head. Fred scrunches up his face and lifts a fist into the air. He makes like he's banging a door with the fist and marches in place. Blue squeezes under Heather's chair and barks. I go inside for more wine and scotch.

On the path to the lake, Blue chases rabbits. They're small and fast and Blue has trouble deciding which one to hunt. If a rabbit darts across the path, left to right, Blue runs hard through low brush until the second rabbit shoots under his nose heading left. Blue brakes, sliding in pine straw, and reroutes with his nose to the ground. By the time the third rabbit jumps across the path, Blue freezes, turning his head side to side, then looks at me. I shrug.

At the lake, Blue jumps in first thing. He swims out fifteen or twenty yards, sniffing and lapping at the surface. Then, as if suddenly realizing the ground has left his feet, Blue jerks a U-turn and paddles fast to shore. He shakes, pants, and lies at my feet. We do this every time.

I fish with a cheap Zebco I bought in town. It's short and light and easy to carry. There's a cartoon picture of Snoopy on the reel. I tie cork, sinker, and hook to the end of the line and dig up worms on the way. The underside of one rock can have enough for an hour. If not, I keep a minnow lure in a box in my pocket. The minnow, red and yellow with reflective stripes, makes a noise like a rattlesnake when I shake it. The googley eyes on his face spin. But the minnow never works. I've only caught fish with worms.

Today, the sun sits fat and hot at the top of the sky. I'm soaked in sweat and hang my shirt from a branch. I wade in knee-deep and cast into the crooks of a fallen tree. Blue rolls on his back at the grassy edge of the shore. I'm watching him when the fish bites. The Snoopy rod doubles over. Line pulls from the reel, singing high and fast. I grab hold and start the fight. But a few seconds and it's done. The fish loops the tree and my hook snags mossy wood. The fish shakes loose and flicks a tail at the surface. Blue runs for the splash. Usually, Blue jumps right in and bites at the water as if the fish is still there. But today, Blue stops short of the fallen tree. He dips his head and sniffs. He begins to whine.

I reel in my line as I walk to the tree. When I get the hook sorted out, I see what Blue sees. A small raccoon, wet and motionless, lies curled up at the waterline. Blue turns a circle and whines.

"Hush, Blue," I say. "No need to cry."

The raccoon looks to be a pound, maybe less. His eyes sit open, unblinking as I nudge him with the tip of my sandal.

"Easy, Blue, I think this one's dead."

Blue lies down with his nose to the raccoon. I can't stop staring either. The glassy eyes and black nose remind me of Blue as a puppy. But it's the paws that get me. I go to my knees and take one between my finger and thumb. It's too much, so I stand up and look at the lake. Three teenage girls walk along the opposite side with lawn chairs and beach towels.

"Sorry, buddy," I say.

But it won't leave me and I sling the fishing pole into the lake. The girls are setting up their chairs and stripping down to bathing suits. They look up, suddenly embarrassed, and clutch towels to their chests. I jump back from the water and run with Blue to the trail.

I wake up at two a.m., cold with night sweats. Heather sleeps on her back, her head ticking side to side and her lips mouthing words I can't understand. I slip out and walk downstairs. Blue stays put, curled in a ball at the foot of the bed. His eyes follow me as I go. In the kitchen, I take a Coke from the fridge and carry it to the garage. Thin squares of moonshine slant through the garage door windows, and in this indigo light, the bed looks finished. The beams and bun feet seem evenly spaced, correctly sized, and precisely joined. The stain seems rich and consistent. The headboard, tall and wide and topped with crown molding, almost looks like the wall of an English billiards room. There are no drawers, and even if there were, there are no rubbers to fill them with. I never started the carving. I knew I would fail.

But right now, in this light, the bed is beautiful. I pad along the edge of the room, toeing boxes and stepping on screws. I retrieve a bottle of Johnnie Walker scotch from under the top tray of my tool box. Then I pull the magazine page from the wall. I backtrack to the kitchen for the phone and sit at the dining room table. I don't even open the Coke. Instead, I take a shot of scotch from the bottle and read the bottom margin: *To place an order, call 1-800-762-1005, 24 hrs/ day, 7 days/ wk.* So I call. I'm given an automated greeting and put on hold. *Your call will be taken in the order in which it was received.* I wonder who else finds themselves in need of Sutter-style furniture at two o'clock in the morning. I stare at the vanilla orchid, noticing that more blooms have opened, and think that maybe two o'clock in the morning is exactly the time at which a person finds himself in need of a good bed.

Blue appears in the kitchen, and it's his clicking paws that remind me of a dog I used to know. A dog who slept under the bed when I lived in Virginia. My dead father's bed. It was a mahogany Hepplewhite with slender posts, hand-carved rosettes and beading. I could have sold it for five-thousand dollars, but the thought of taking money made me sick. It looked ridiculous even after I tore off the drapery. Nothing felt right about sleeping in it, if I could sleep at all.

And then there's the girl who became my wife, who became my ex-wife, who slept in that bed. Not to mention the bastard who bought it. So when I packed my bags, I left the bed where it stood.

Blue licks my hand. A cool draft floats in from the garage, sending chills down my back. I spill drops of scotch on the table, beading up like dew. I take another swallow. It won't be long now before summer is over.

A bright-voiced woman clicks on the line.

"How can I help you this evening?"

"I want a bed," I say. I pluck an open flower from the orchid and hold it to my nose. I am stupidly surprised to discover the bloom does, in fact, smell like vanilla. I wipe my eyes.

"Is there a particular style I can help you with?" she asks.

"Yes," I say. "Sutter-style panel bed. Crown molding, bun feet, mortis-and-tenon joinery."

"Size?"

"Queen. No, wait. King."

"Excellent choice. How will you be paying this evening?"

"Credit."

"That'll be fine, sir. I just need to take down some information."

"Of course," I say.

Then I tell her everything.

EPILOGUE:

AFTER EVERYTHING

B efore I am beaten to death by men I do not know in a bar called the Black Oyster, there is one other thing of importance I do. I have shaved my beard, thin and grizzly gray, and I have traveled to Barlo, Alabama. The red clay roads have been named now, a federal mandate following September 11, and so I turn on Kentucky drive without having to squint to see the rusted license plate nailed to a tree. I pass the Erebus graveyard, the death masks gone green with mold, and I pretend they do not frighten me. Just for today, I am sober. I make the cabin before sunset and park in front of the skinning shed. I get out of the car, and for what seems like years, I stand there, slack jawed and staring. Not one thing has changed. The cabin, of course, looks very different—new wood, new tin roof, new porch on the south wall. I suppose they couldn't salvage much after the fire. But the skinning shed hasn't been touched. Dozens of antlers nailed to the frame, some so old they have insect holes bored deep into the bone. I break the spell by taking a step closer, looking carefully to find my ten-point. It's there, nailed to the far post, a bit of Spanish moss hanging from the tines. I reach up and grab it with both hands. I pull it free, the nails slipping easily from the now rotten wood.

Under the cabin, I find the Lester canoe. There were no

cars in the drive, so I put in right here at the dock. I paddle out slow. One smooth stroke at a time. My still-strong arms remembering the pattern as if I'd been out yesterday. One smooth stroke at a time. The sun dips into the tree tops and shadows streak out across the lake. I keep paddling. Past the island where we found deer bones when we were kids. Past the inlet where Dad would drop anchor and drink. I paddle to the dam, a mound of bulldozed dirt covered in thick grass marked by alligator trails, and tie to a fallen hemlock. I walk over the rise and down to the swamp, the real swamp, the swamp my great grandfather dammed to build this lake so long ago. I slip a pint of Wild Turkey bourbon from my pocket and take one bitter swallow. I crouch down when the water comes over my boots and pour the rest into the swamp. I sit on my heels, dark water soaking into my pants, almost to the waist. I reach out with the antlers, holding them out over deeper water, letting the skull plate submerge. I hold it there, with the ten points rising up, white and chalky and dry.

I hold it there until my legs begin to shake, my hands grow weary, and my eyesight begins to fail. I hold it there until I can no longer stand it. Then I let them go.

MURRAY DUNLAP's work has appeared in *Virginia Quarterly Review, Post Road, Night Train, Silent Voices, The Bark, SmokeLong Quarterly, The Smoking Poet*, and many others. His stories have been twice nominated for the Pushcart Prize, as well as Best New American Voices. His first book, *Alabama*, was a finalist for the Maurice Prize in Fiction. Murray also served as co-editor of *What Doesn't Kill You...* (Press 53), an anthology of stories about struggle.

A NOTE FROM THE AUTHOR

I would like to thank first, in a semi-chronological way, my teachers: Beverly Davis, Michael Knight, Fred Ashe, Laura Dave, Jim White, Pam Houston, and Lucy Corin. I would also like to thank a few special editors: Rusty Barnes, Meg Pokrass, Claudia Kawczynska, Shelagh Watkins, Kevin Watson, and Mary Cotton. But most important of all, I want to thank my mother, without whom so many things would not be at all possible, much less this book (*Thanks, Mom!*).

M.D.